Condolence Casseroles

By

J Lee Mitchell

Condolence Casseroles

By J Lee Mitchell

First Edition

Cover design by Mariah Sinclair & Associates
www.mariahsinclair.com.

Dedication

To all my family. Thank you for telling and inspiring the best stories. I love you all more than you will ever know.

TABLE OF CONTENTS

Chapter 1

Q'Bita woke up confused. She had no idea where she was, or how she'd gotten there. Her head throbbed, and she was thirsty. As the cobwebs started to clear, she realized she was in the hospital and vaguely remembered falling.

A soft snore made her turn her head. Andy sat stuffed into a small chair a few inches from her bed. At six foot four this was no easy feat, and he looked uncomfortable. Fortunately Andy was one of those people who could sleep anywhere.

Q'Bita had learned early in their relationship that there were three things Andy Hansen loved: sleeping, fishing, and pie. As she reached out to touch his arm, the glint of her new engagement ring caught her eye and a wave of emotion washed over her as she realized she could now officially add herself to the list of things Andy loved.

The warm fuzzy feeling was short-lived, as the events of the previous few hours came rushing back to her all at once, like a movie playing on fast-forward. Andy's rescue, the shootout, cops everywhere, Henri on a gurney handing her a phone, being at the ER with Andy, then Alain's voice on the phone, then everything going black.

"What the hell?"

Q'Bita hadn't meant for her words to come out quite so loud. Andy jumped and almost toppled out of the little chair.

"Q'Bita! You're awake. How do you feel? Should I get the doctor? God, you scared the hell out of me."

"Andy, slow down. I'm fine. Well, not fine. When I called Henri's boss, it was Alain that answered the phone. How's that possible? Dead people can't answer phones."

Andy sat back down in the chair and ran his hands through his thick, wavy hair. He stared at her for a few seconds and then spoke softly.

"Q'Bita, it's not possible. You know that. You'd just been through a traumatic experience, you were exhausted, and it's not too much of a stretch to think your mind might not have been processing things clearly. I'm sure there's a reasonable explanation."

Q'Bita lay back against the pillows and closed her eyes. She was sure the voice that answered the phone had been Alain's, but it made no sense. Then a thought occurred to her.

"You're right, I'm being silly. Where's Henri's phone? I'll just call his boss again and then I'll know for sure it isn't Alain, and we can put this to rest."

Andy shifted in his seat and wrinkled up his face.

"Okay, I know how your mind works, so don't take this the wrong way and start dreaming up conspiracy theories—"

"What? Tell me."

"You fainted before you got a chance to tell whoever answered about Henri. By the time I got back to the phone the line was dead. After they got you all settled in the room here, I tried calling again and the number you called has been disconnected."

"Disconnected? Are you sure? That doesn't make sense. How could it work, then be disconnected so soon afterward?"

"I wondered that too, so I called Jamie and he did some digging. Henri's phone and the number you called are both burner phones. Jamie also verified that Henri does work for Interpol, but he's an administrative assistant, not a field agent, and there is no record of a Victor Cortez associated with Interpol. If you ask me, I think your friend Henri may be on the take and this Cortez guy is probably just as dirty as Gianni Marini. If that's the case, I want you as far away from Henri as possible."

Q'Bita's first reaction was to bristle at being scolded like a child. Her second reaction wasn't much better, and two seconds after she started speaking, her mind was telling her mouth to shut-up.

"Why do you always assume that I'm going to do something foolish and that you have to protect me from myself? What have I ever done that would make you think I don't have the common sense to know who I should or shouldn't associate with?"

Andy sat up straight in his chair and stared at her with raised eyebrows. His look conveyed his lack of amusement.

"I'm going to chalk those questions up to you having a concussion, because I know you already know the answer. Correction—answers. The list gets longer by the day."

Q'Bita flopped back against her pillows and sighed.

"Okay, fine. Maybe I've made a few poor choices over the last few months but you're wrong about Henri. He could easily have outed me and Jamie but he didn't. He sacrificed himself, and now he's the one—"

Q'Bita's emotions overwhelmed her and she couldn't finish. Andy sat back and she could see his expression soften.

"Okay, babe, maybe you're right. Maybe Henri isn't the bad guy, but until he pulls through and I get a chance to talk to him I'd prefer it if you just steered clear of him and his boss. We still don't know what kind of situation we're dealing with here, and it could be dangerous."

Q'Bita was too tired to argue with him any further, so she just nodded her head in agreement.

"Has there been any update on Henri's condition?"

"I haven't left your side since you fell, so I'm not sure. Why don't you get some rest and I'll go check on Henri?"

Andy stood to leave but Q'Bita reached out towards him. He smiled and stepped closer to the bed. She motioned for him to lean down, then reached up and hugged him.

"I'm sorry. I didn't mean what I said. I love that you want to protect me, and I appreciate everything you do for me."

Andy kissed the top of her head, then her lips.

"I'm sorry too. Now get some rest. I'll be back in a little while to check on you."

Q'Bita lay back and closed her eyes. She tried pushing all memories of the last few hours out of her mind, but it was hopeless. Her thoughts were stuck on an endless loop of gunfire and Alain's voice.

After a while, Q'Bita sat up and looked around the room for a phone but didn't see one. She eased her legs over the side of the bed and immediately felt the room start to spin. She closed her eyes, but that just made things worse. She was just settling back into bed when she heard the door open.

Q'Bita turned to see Beecher and Rene entering the room.

"Sweet honey on a biscuit, that is one angry-looking goose egg. Luckily for you, I brought three shades of concealer and some BB cream. I'll do what I can with your hair, but even I have my limitations."

"What's wrong with my hair?" Q'Bita asked defensively.

"Don't answer that," Beecher said to Rene.

3

Rene rolled his eyes and pushed Beecher aside.

"Q'Bita deserves the truth. That mop of curls looks like an Airedale Terrier in an electrical storm."

"Seriously? Dear God. Get me a mirror."

"Q'Bita, pay no attention to him. He's being dramatic."

Rene plopped an oversized Versace handbag onto her bed and dug inside until he found a mirror. Q'Bita gasped when she saw the pale, wild-haired person staring back at her."

"Rene, give it a rest. Q'Bita's had a rough night."

"I'm just saying, they shear sheep for less."

Q'Bita lightly touched the large lump above her right eye and shrunk back in pain.

"Rene's right, Beecher. I look horrible."

"Considering everything you've been through in the last few days, I think you've earned a free pass."

"You don't know the half of it."

Q'Bita spent the next ten minutes explaining everything that had happened from the time she'd left the Red Herring Inn with Jamie and Hadleigh until she'd woken in the hospital. When she finished, Beecher let out a low whistle and Rene was staring at her with his mouth open wide.

"My logical side knows it couldn't possibly have been Alain that answered, but the side of me that never really got closure won't stop obsessing over it."

"Maybe he has a twin. Oh wait, maybe it's a clone, or a doppelganger."

"Rene, don't be ridiculous. There is no such thing as a doppelganger."

Rene looked down his nose at Beecher and dismissed him with a flutter of his hand.

"This from a man who traipses around the woods in the dead of the night looking for Bigfoot."

"Beecher's right, Rene. No such things as doppelgangers, but squatches are definitely real," Andy said as he entered the room.

"Be warned, Q'Bita. Marry a man who believes in Bigfoot and next thing you know you'll be spending your Sunday afternoons scouring back country roads looking for roadkill while he tries to convince you that raccoon penis bones are made of ivory."

"It's called a baculum, and they sell like crazy online," Beecher replied.

"Round these parts, the old timers used them for toothpicks or to stir their coffee," Andy said.

Rene's nostrils flared and he made a gagging sound.

"If either of you makes a dick-pic joke, I'm going to slap you senseless."

Q'Bita was too busy laughing to worry about her hair or her goose egg. Once they'd gotten it all out of their system, Andy walked over and sat in the small chair beside her bed. He reached out and took her hand, and gave it a gentle kiss.

"How's Henri?" Q'Bita asked.

"He lost a lot of blood and he's still unconscious, but the surgeon says he's a fighter and they think he'll pull through."

A wave of relief washed over Q'Bita as she sank back into her pillows. She closed her eyes and listened to her brother, Rene, and Andy talking until their voices faded away and she was fast asleep.

Chapter 2

The doctor came in early the next morning to release Q'Bita. He gave her strict orders to take it easy for a few days, and Andy promised that he'd personally see to it that she obeyed doctor's orders. So far Andy had kept his promise, and Q'Bita was beginning to wonder just how much longer she'd be treated like a helpless, wounded female before Andy simmered down. The wheelchair ride from her room to the parking lot was bad enough, but lifting her into his truck and buckling her in was a bit much. She knew his heart was in the right place, but she was ready to get back to her normal routine as soon as they reached the Red Herring Inn.

As they pulled into the driveway a thought struck her.

"Oh my gosh! Allegro. I almost forgot about the little guy. Did Jamie and Hadleigh bring him back yet?"

"Q'Bita, you're supposed to be taking it easy. I'm sure they can handle taking care of a puppy for a few more days."

"Andy, I appreciate your concern but I'm fine. Besides, I can't wait to cuddle him. He's so cute."

Andy shook his head and gave her a disapproving look.

"Q'Bita… Don't get too attached. Sooner or later Gianni Marini is going to notice his dog is missing and want him back."

"Gianni Marini is a criminal and he told his goon to kill you. I doubt he's going anywhere any time soon."

"That's true, but that doesn't mean we can just keep his dog. I'm sure he will want to have someone come pick up Allegro eventually."

Q'Bita bit down on her bottom lip and sighed. Andy was right. Allegro was not just any puppy, he was a highly trained truffle hunter and worth a great deal to whoever owned him.

She unbuckled her seatbelt and moved to open the door but stopped when Andy reached for her arm.

"Sit still. I'll come around and help you."

"Andy, I'm fine. It's a bump on the head, not a debilitating injury."

Andy smiled so wide he could have swallowed a chicken.

"I know, but I like how you scrunch up your face to keep from telling me off when I try to carry you."

"You're an evil man, Andy Hansen."

"Evil and hungry. Any chance you got some pie stashed away somewhere?"

On the way inside, Q'Bita let Andy wrap an arm around her. She wasn't about to admit that she was still a little dizzy and her legs felt weak.

When they got inside, Q'Bita was surprised to see her mother wearing her apron and rolling out pie crust.

"Oh, baby, you're home. Come here and let me hug you."

Her mother wiped her flour-coated hands on the apron and rushed toward Q'Bita with arms open wide. "I'm so glad you're okay. You scared us almost to death."

"Not my intent, I promise," Q'Bita said with a chuckle.

"So, what kind of pie are you making, Kari?" Andy asked.

"Don't get yourself too excited, Andrew. It's chicken pot pie, and it's for tonight's class."

"Oh crap, I completely forgot. That class is almost fully booked. We need to get moving or we'll never be ready in time."

"By we, I hope you mean your mother, Evie, and myself, because word on the street is that you're under doctor's orders to rest. You're welcome to pop a squat on a stool behind the counter and look pretty but under no circumstances will you be teaching this evening."

Q'Bita opened her mouth to protest but her nana gave her the do-not-sass-me look. Growing up, Q'Bita and Beecher had learned the hard way to never push it when Nana gave them the look. It was a fast track to an ear-boxing for sure.

Q'Bita felt Andy's hand on her shoulder and turned to face him.

"I have an idea. Why don't we take the class together?"

"Andy, you're sweet but it's a hands-on class. You'd have to wear an apron and roll out crust before you'd get to eat."

Q'Bita saw her mother smiling and trying not to giggle out loud.

"I'm not sure what you ladies find so amusing. I'm perfectly secure in my manhood, and I think it would be fun. Besides, you spend an awful lot of time trying to do my job. Maybe it's time you get a little taste of your own medicine," Andy jabbed back with a smile.

Q'Bita wasn't sure if she should hug him or slug him for being a smartass but the thought of him in an apron and covered in flour had a certain appeal that she couldn't resist.

"Okay then, it's settled. I'll call Rene and see if you can borrow one of his aprons."

"Rene? I was thinking maybe I could borrow a bar-b-que apron from your dad."

The look of horror on Andy's face was priceless, and neither Q'Bita nor her mother could hold back their laughter.

Their fun at Andy's expense was cut short by the sound of a commotion coming from the kitchen garden.

Q'Bita rushed outside with Andy right behind her. She noticed Jamie and Rene at the edge of the garden and could hear barking and hissing coming from her lavender patch.

"Oh, thank God. Quick, Andy, use your Taser, or lethal force if you have to. That beast is going to rend my poor Rolfie limb from limb."

"Calm down, Rene. Allegro is a puppy; he just wants to play," Jamie snapped.

"Play? Does that look like playing to you? He's snarling and foaming at the mouth. I think he's rabid."

"He's not foaming at the mouth, Rene. He's drooling. Dogs do that when they're overly excited."

"No, they hump things when they're excited. So don't just stand there looking like your parents shared a gene pool. Go retrieve that beast before I have to teach Rolfie about safe words."

Q'Bita rolled her eyes at Andy and he shrugged his shoulders at her.

"You two are ridiculous," Q'Bita chided as she stepped into the garden and picked up Allegro.

Allegro immediately forgot about Rolfie and started drowning Q'Bita in kisses and nipping at her fingers.

"Hello, handsome. I see we're going to have to teach you some manners," Q'Bita cooed as she scratched the rambunctious puppy behind his ear.

"Please don't tell me that hell spawn will be freeloading here long enough to be taught anything."

"Don't worry, Rene, sooner or later I'm sure Gianni Marini will want his property back, and Rolfie can reclaim his rightful spot as master of the manor," Andy said dryly.

"Property? If I didn't know better, I'd say you had something against puppies."

"Q'Bita, I have nothing against puppies. I'm against watching you get attached to something that you're just going to have to give back. I don't want to see you get your heart broken, that's all."

Q'Bita felt a little stab of pain move through her chest as she snuggled her face into Allegro's fur again. She was already attached and didn't want to think about having to give him up. Allegro squirmed and wiggled in her arms as Rolfie made his way out of the lavender and paused to give her a look that implied he disapproved of her attachment to Allegro as much as Andy did.

"Ha, I think Rolfie just gave you the stink eye, Q'B-Doll."

"Rolfie's very intuitive, practically an empath, and he knows a traitor when he sees one."

"Traitor? Well, we'll see how he feels when it's time for cream. My guess is that all will be forgiven as soon as I sit the bowl down in front of him."

"Perhaps. Or you may just find that your betrayal has tainted the cream and Rolfie will decide to take his afternoon repast elsewhere."

Q'Bita laughed as Andy turned to Jamie with a confused look on his face. "What the hell is a repast? Am I the only one who has no idea what Rene is carrying on about most of the time?"

"Okay, you three, I think it's time we all go get some coffee and something to eat. My head hurts and my stomach is growling."

"I vote for pie."

"Of course you do," Q'Bita said as she held Allegro out towards Andy. "Take him while I wade out of this lavender."

Allegro looked like a tiny toy in Andy's arms. He snuggled against Andy's chest, yawned, then closed his eyes. Q'Bita could see Andy's whole posture change as he cradled the puppy. Gone was the stick-straight, serious lawman, and in his place was a gentle giant who'd just been won over to Team Puppy.

Chapter 3

The sound of thunder woke Q'Bita from her nap. Allegro stirred in her lap then decided to return to napping without Q'Bita. She checked her cell phone and saw a text from Jamie. "Come find me when you wake up."

She checked the time and was surprised to see that Jamie had sent the text more than an hour ago. She'd never been a napper, and couldn't believe she'd slept that long or that Andy had left her alone that long. As much as she loved him and cherished their alone time, she had been relieved when he suggested she rest while he went into town to talk to Mike Collins.

She sat for a few minutes listening to the sound of the approaching storm and petting Allegro's soft fur. He stirred again and nuzzled her hand with his snout. She gave it a gentle scratch and laughed as he nipped at her fingers. "Okay, buddy, I guess we'd better get you outside to handle some business before the rain gets here."

She tucked the small dog under her arm and headed for the front desk. Jamie was checking in an older couple in matching rain slickers. She hung back until they left the counter for their room.

"There you are. What took you so long?"

"We were napping. Chasing cats is exhausting."

"I'm sure it is." Jamie's reply held an edge of sarcasm that caught her off guard.

"What has you so worked up?"

"Sorry, Q'B-Doll. It's been a rough few days and I think I need some sleep. I make hacking look easy but it's nerve-wracking trying to get in and out without getting caught, and I'm out of practice. Not to mention the almost getting killed part."

A wave of guilt rolled over Q'Bita and she realized just how much she'd asked of her best friend.

"I'm sorry, Jamie, I should never have dragged you into this."

Jamie shot her a raised eyebrow and snorted. "Like I would have stayed out of it even if you'd insisted. You're my sister from another Nana. I'll always have your back, girl."

Q'Bita felt herself getting weepy.

"Okay, kill the waterworks. We've got bigger problems to deal with."

"Bigger? I don't think that's possible."

"I'm sure the hunky lawman told you that he had me do some digging into Henri's boss and I came up empty."

"Ya, I thought that was weird. The whole thing seems suspicious to me."

"It's suspicious alright. Check this out," Jamie said as he handed her the reservation log for the day.

Q'Bita gasped when she saw the third name from the top of the list.

"Victor Cortez? This can't be a coincidence."

"Damn right it's not. That reservation was made less than an hour after you placed your call, and get this, it came from an unregistered number, but I was able to trace it back to Lyon, France."

"Lyon? That's where Interpol headquarters is."

"Exactly. Gianni Marini may be in custody, but I don't think this mess is over yet."

Q'Bita stared at the reservation log for a few seconds, trying to make sense of everything, but it was no use. Her brain was still a little scrambled from the concussion.

"Have you told Andy yet?"

"Not yet. I wasn't sure if you'd want me to or not."

"To be honest, I'm not sure what I want. Part of me wants to be honest and call him right now, but what if he just dismisses this as a coincidence and tells me to drop it?"

"Ha. We both know you're not going to drop it. Besides, he should know you well enough by now to realize that your gut is usually right. If you think something's up, it probably is."

Q'Bita's mind was racing and she was lost in thought until Allegro finally started squirming and yipping.

"Do you want me to take him?" Jamie asked.

"No, I'm okay. The fresh air will do me some good. Can you come with us?"

"Sure. Give me a sec to tell Julie I'm taking a break. I'll meet you on the porch."

The wind had picked up as the storm approached, and Q'Bita could feel the moisture in the air. She set Allegro down and watched him make a beeline for the grass. Jamie appeared beside her and handed her an umbrella. "I thought you might need this. If that storm hits while we're out here, I won't be able to tell you and Allegro apart. You'll just be two balls of wet, fuzzy curls."

"I'm the one with the bluish-purple head wound and the dry nose."

"Got ya. Now let's go figure out what to do about Victor Cortez."

As they reached the bottom step, a huge clap of thunder rang out, causing Q'Bita's heart to skip a beat. She said a silent prayer that it wasn't a portent of things to come.

***

When his flight finally arrived in Charleston, he was the first one off the plane. He found the closest available exit and started lighting his cigarette before the doors even swished open.

A wave of humidity rolled over him as soon as he exited the airport. It had rained recently, and the air was now as thick as syrup. The flight had been pleasant, but this weather not so much. He would never understand why his wife had chosen to leave Spain and come to this place. He knew his death would upset her, but he never imagined she'd do something so irrational so soon after he was gone.

He took another deep drag and dropped the butt on the ground next to the ashtray can then ducked back into the air-conditioned terminal. The bags were just now making their way to the luggage carousel. He waited as patiently as possible for his bag to appear then snagged it off the line and headed for the rental car counter.

His first stop would be to check on Henri. On the way he'd call Monique and have her find him somewhere else to stay. He knew he couldn't avoid Q'Bita much longer, but he wasn't ready to come back from the dead just yet.

Chapter 4

Jamie sent Q'Bita a text early the next morning, letting her know that the mysterious Victor Cortez had arrived in the middle of the night and requested to not be disturbed. The night staff clerk described Victor as handsome but didn't have much else to say. Q'Bita was disappointed to learn that the clerk had also been so busy flirting that she'd forgotten to get a copy of Victor's ID. Q'Bita would now have to wait and check him out in person.

She wasn't proud of the fact that she'd tricked Andy into going to town to pick up the meat order for the evening class, but she knew he'd be glued to her all morning and she wouldn't get a chance to check out Victor with Andy around.

Q'Bita spent the first part of the morning stalking the hall outside Victor's room but he failed to make an appearance. She'd even gone so far as to set a pot of fresh coffee just outside the door, hoping the aroma would draw him out, but that was a bust. She finally gave up around 10:30 and made her way to the kitchen.

***

"So, who's this guest you're so worked up over? Is he some sort of celebrity or something?" Evie asked.

"No, just someone I'm curious about, is all," Q'Bita replied.

"Girl, please. Who do you think you're talking to? You're full of more butt nuggets than those dreadful chickens Beecher's always fawning over. Spill your dirty little secret or I'll have Evie torture it out of you."

Q'Bita shook her head and laughed at her brother-in-law. His drama knob was set to full power today, and he wasn't about to run out of batteries any time soon.

"How about we focus on getting lunch ready before we have a porch full of hungry hunters to deal with?"

"Hunters, my ass." Evie cackled. "That bunch has no business calling themselves hunters. Hunters actually bag something. This is just a bunch of fools chasing an imaginary creature around the woods. They only thing they're going to catch is a damn cold."

"Now, Evie, don't let my husband hear you say Bigfoot isn't real."

"Rene's right, Evie. Beecher takes his cryptid creatures very seriously," Q'Bita added as she pulled a tray of cookies out of the oven and sat them on the counter to cool.

Rene took one look at the cookies and was off on a tangent again.

"I fail to comprehend how an entire group of grown-ass men can waste a perfectly good weekend traipsing around the forest looking for some seven-foot-tall, hairy-chested beast, and think that anyone is going to take them seriously."

"I'm not sure why they're wasting their time looking for you in the woods either, Rene," Evie teased.

"You know damn well that I am religious about having this finely chiseled specimen waxed weekly."

"Is that before or after poor Sadie waxes your keister and man parts?"

Q'Bita wasn't a prude but this conversation was escalating a little too quickly for her.

"Okay, you two, TMI. Let's refocus. We've got a planning committee about to descend on our porch, and I want to make sure we feed them before they have time to move past Bigfoot and on to snallygasters or crocodingos."

"Croco-what? Wait, never mind. Unless Gucci makes it into a purse in this season Pantone, I don't really care."

"You will when Beecher decides to have it stuffed and hung on your living room wall, you big tulip."

It frustrated Q'Bita to no end when Evie and Rene started on each other and ignored her plea to get back to work, but the look of horror on Rene's face at the thought of taxidermy as décor was so priceless, she couldn't stay angry at either of them.

***

Beecher appeared about twenty minutes later to check on lunch, and snagged a cookie from the tray. Rene slapped playfully at his hand.

"What? They're so cute I can't help myself."

"Cute? You think they look cute? I'm suffering from hand-cramping after piping all that fur onto their little gingerbread men bodies so they would look realistic, which was no easy feat, considering there's no such thing as Bigfoot."

"You said no easy feat. Get it? Feet, like Bigfoot."

"Your humor is lost on me. Now stay out of my cookies until they make it to the porch. Oh, and you'd better make sure your burly hunter friends know who made these. I don't want them thinking I don't support my man."

Q'Bita tried hard not to laugh at Rene's feigned outrage. He had put a lot of work into the Bigfoot cookies, and she had to give him credit—they looked amazing. They put the finishing touches on lunch and started loading up the trays.

"Evie, you give that tray to Beecher. It's too heavy," Q'Bita said sternly.

"You don't need to worry yourself about me, missy. I'm having a good day today and I can manage just fine."

Q'Bita watched as Evie picked up the tray with steady hands and started for the porch. They'd all been worried about Evie since she had recently been diagnosed with a mild case of essential tremors. She'd had good days and bad recently, but her pride often led to her concealing which days were which. Q'Bita had promised her nana that she would keep an eye on Evie and not let her overdo it when Liddy Lou wasn't there to do it herself.

The porch full of hungry men quickly polished off every morsel of lunch and were making their way through Rene's Bigfoot cookies just as fast. Q'Bita moved about the tables, refilling everyone's glass with iced tea. She loved listening to her brother and his friends talk about their hunting adventures. They tended to take their hunting very seriously, but they were on a not-so-serious roll today.

"I'm telling you, Beecher, it was a Bigfoot."

Jake Morgan was trying to convince them he'd been shaken out of his tree stand last week by a Bigfoot. More likely Jake had fallen asleep, or had too much to drink, and fell out, but she'd keep that thought to herself and let him tell his version.

"A Bigfoot, ya say. I don't suppose you got a picture of this magnificent beast, did you, Jake?"

"You can mock me all ya want, Orvis, but I'm telling you the God's honest truth. It was terrifying to come that close to the Devil's monkey. If Beau wouldn't have scared it off, it would probably have torn me limb from limb and dragged my carcass off to its den."

"Oh, for feck's sake, Jake. That hound of yours is a hundred years old and wouldn't drag its fat ass off the porch if a pack of squirrels were stealing your tractor out of the front yard."

"He's just avoiding your question, Orvis," Cane Jessop weighed in.

"Is that so? I can't imagine why Jake would want to do that, unless there's something Jake doesn't want us to know."

Cane Jessop and Orvis were baiting Jake. They knew exactly why he wasn't answering.

"You two just keep running your traps and thinking you're so smart. Once you see Hank's video you won't be acting so high and mighty," Jake bit back.

"I keep hearing all about this video but I ain't run across anyone that's actually seen it yet," Cane replied.

"Your Uncle Put's seen it," Jake said.

"That so? Well, I guess I'll have to stop over there later this week and ask him all about it, then."

"I'm sure you'll manage to show your ugly mug right before dinner, too," Evie teased.

"Aunt Evie, you know I'd never do something so devious as to plan my visit around your cooking… unless you're making venison stew and homemade bread. Then all bets are off."

Q'Bita laughed as Evie planted her hands on her hips and tried to look annoyed, but it was pointless. Everyone in Castle Creek knew that Put and Evie had no children of their own and they doted on their nephew.

The sound of someone clearing their throat drew everyone's attention. Q'Bita turned toward the sound and noticed Clarity Fessler sitting on the far side of the porch, next to Orvis. Clarity had been so quiet Q'Bita hadn't noticed she was there.

The pause in the conversation was awkward, and Q'Bita noticed Clarity blushing.

"I'm sorry to interrupt but my lunch break is almost over and I need to get back to work. Is there anything else we need to discuss about the hunt planning? I'd hate to miss anything important." Q'Bita made her way over closer to Clarity and started to refill her glass. "Oh, no, thank you, Miss Block. I really do have to get back to work."

"Please, call me Q'Bita. I have to say, I'm surprised to see you here. I wouldn't have pegged you as a hunter."

Clarity laughed shyly. "I majored in biology with a minor in cryptozoology. My interest is purely scientific. One of the reasons I came here to Castle Creek to do my grad work was because of your diversity of wildlife. I hope to someday become the leading expert on animal wound identification. I joined this group because I figure sooner or later one of these guys is going to get bit, or worse, and it will be good research."

She'd said that last part without so much as a smile and Q'Bita made a mental note to ask Andy more about his favorite lab tech. She'd always seemed so sweet and shy to Q'Bita, but this side of her was kind of scary.

Chapter 5

After lunch, they made quick work of the cleanup and Q'Bita sent Evie home to rest. Unlike Evie, Rene had needed no prodding to go take a nap, and he headed home with Beecher as soon as the last cookie was gone. Q'Bita was enjoying the peace and quiet.

She checked her phone and saw a text from Jamie. "Any progress on operation Victor?"

"Nothing yet, but I have a plan."

A few seconds later her phone rang.

"Spill it, sister."

"Hello to you too, Jamie."

"Cut the chit-chat and let's hear your plan. My shift starts in two hours and I need to determine if I have to come in early to bail you out or not."

"You're starting to sound like Rene."

Q'Bita could hear Jamie drumming his fingers on something impatiently as he waited for her to tell him what she was thinking.

"Okay, okay. I'm going to go get Allegro and just stop by Victor's room and introduce myself. I'll tell him that we do that for all our guests. I'm hoping that Allegro will be so cute and distracting that he glosses over the fact that I'm technically invading his privacy."

"Huh, not a bad plan. Lacks some of the intrigue and action-movie drama I was expecting but your way sounds like it might work too."

"What where you expecting? Did you think I was going to strap on a body harness and drop out of the air duct or sling-shot myself though his window à la Mission Impossible?"

"Now that's a plan with some style. Don't forget the all-leather cat suit and the thigh-high spike-heeled boots."

"All I'd need to complete that look is an eye mask and cat ears."

"I don't know, Q'B-Doll. You're more bunny ears, I think."

"Very funny. Okay, I gotta go. I have a mystery guest to welcome."

***

Q'Bita took a few minutes to smooth her hair and reapply her lipstick. She dabbed some more concealer on her bruised forehead and took a deep, calming breath. She wasn't sure what or whom she expected to find by confronting Victor, but she knew she wouldn't be able to put this behind her until she was certain that the voice she'd heard on the other end of the phone had not been Alain's.

It wasn't just the sound of the voice that had unnerved her, it was the thousand tiny memories that came rushing back to her when she heard it. A shiver ran through her whole body just thinking about it, even now.

"Pull it together, Q'Bita. You're being silly," she said to herself out loud. She dabbed on some perfume and decided it was now or never. "You can do this," she reminded herself.

Allegro was waiting for her by the door, looking as adorable as ever. She scooped him up and he wiggled excitedly in her arms.

"Okay, boy, calm down. We have a mission to accomplish first, then we'll go find you a snack in the kitchen." The little dog yelped in agreement as if he'd actually understood what she was saying. She snuggled him close to her and felt herself relax a little. It was strange what a calming effect he had on her, and she knew she was already too attached to him, but that was an issue she'd have to deal with at a later date.

The trip from her suite to Victor's room only took a few seconds, and she was in front of his door sooner than she'd hoped. The Do Not Disturb sign was gone, and the coffee pot was now sitting empty on the serving tray, along with a note. She bent down and picked up the note, and felt her hands shake as she read the simple reply, "Merci beaucoup." She wasn't sure if she was imagining it or not but the handwriting looked very similar to Alain's.

She took another deep breath and knocked on the door. A few seconds passed and no one answered. She leaned closer to the door and knocked again, hoping to hear someone moving around inside.

"You just missed him."

The unexpected voice behind Q'Bita startled her, and she jumped. When she turned around, she saw the elderly man she'd watched checking in with his wife in their matching rain slickers.

"Sorry, dear, didn't mean to scare you. He just left about five minutes

19

ago. Nice fella, funny accent. Seemed to be in a hurry though, said he had an appointment to get to."

Q'Bita shifted Allegro to her other side and reached out to shake the man's hand.

"Thank you. I'm Q'Bita Block, one of the owners here at the Red Herring Inn. How are you and your wife enjoying your stay?"

The man smiled and gave her a firm hand shake. "Harper Collins, but my friends call me Harp. Pleased to make your acquaintance, Miss Block. My Elizabeth and I are having a wonderful stay so far. Quite the place you have here. I understand this is a family-run business. If you're one of the owners, then you must be related to Liddy Lou Cormier."

"Yes. She's my grandmother. Do you know her?" Q'Bita asked, surprised.

"Oh yes, dear. We go way back."

Q'Bita caught a hint of sadness in his expression and his tone.

"Elizabeth and I were so hoping to catch a small visit with her while we were here, if it isn't too much trouble."

"Of course. I'm sure she'd be delighted to see you. She spent the night in Charleston on some personal business but she's due back this evening. I'll tell her that you're here as soon as I see her."

"Thank you, that would be much appreciated. It was nice meeting you, dear. I'll let you get back to your business then." The man reached out and ruffled Allegro's fur then shuffled down the hall and disappeared down the stairs.

Q'Bita stood watching him go and then turned back toward Victor's door. She made a snap decision that she hoped she wouldn't regret later. She pulled her master key from her pocket and slid it into the door. There was a small beep and then a click. She turned the handle and pushed the door open a crack.

"Hello? Anyone in?" she called quietly.

When no one answered and there was no sign of movement from within, she pushed the door open further and slipped inside the room. A faint trace of cologne still hung in the air, and she froze as she realized it was the same cologne that Alain had worn. Allegro sneezed, and it made her laugh at herself. She was being ridiculous; cologne wasn't specific to one person. It was a popular brand, and she was sure lots of men wore the same scent. She edged slowly into the room, set Allegro down, and looked about, wondering where to start.

***

Alain cursed as he hit every bump in the little dirt road leading from the Red Herring Inn to the main road. His nerves and patience were both completely shot. Henri was in much worse shape than he'd expected, he still had to figure out how to convince the local cops to release Gianni Marini into his custody, and worst of all was the fact that a ridiculous Bigfoot Festival meant that there wasn't another room available anywhere but the Red Herring Inn, which made it almost impossible to conceal himself from Q'Bita for much longer.

He reached for his phone and cursed again as he realized it was still sitting on the nightstand of his room. He swung the car around and headed back to the Red Herring Inn, hoping this wasn't a sign of just how badly this was all going to end.

As he pulled into the front drive of the Red Herring Inn, he saw Beecher standing near the front steps, tossing feed to a small flock of chickens. It had been several years since they'd last seen each other but Alain wasn't about to risk being recognized. He followed the circular drive around to the back and parked near the barn. He had scouted out a back stairway right after he'd arrived and had used it to slip in and out undetected so far.

Alain scanned the grounds and didn't see anyone around. He moved quickly to the door and ducked inside. He moved quietly up the stairs to the second floor and paused on the landing. He listened for a few seconds, and when he was sure no one else was in the hallway, he walked quickly to his room.

He reached for his room key and then froze as he noticed the door was already open. He put his ear to the open door and could hear the faint sound of someone moving around inside. His mind shuffled rapidly through the various possibilities. Was he being robbed? Did Marini know he had set him up and so had sent someone after him? Both seemed unlikely. He chided himself for being so paranoid. He was, after all, a trained agent.

He reached down, pulled the small handgun from his ankle holster, and slipped silently through the door. Whoever was in there had chosen

21

the wrong man to mess with today.

***

Q'Bita started with the closet. Everything was hung up meticulously according to color and looked to be expensive. Whoever this guy was, he was obviously a neat freak with good taste in clothing. She moved on to the medicine cabinet next, but it contained just the typical male grooming stuff. So far nothing telling, and she was beginning to feel guilty for invading this man's privacy. She was just about to take Allegro and go when she spotted the cell phone on the night stand. She chewed on the corner of her lip for a few seconds, trying to decide if she should look though it or not. The temptation was too much, and she couldn't stop herself.

She sat down on the edge of the bed, picked up the phone, and it lit up. She swiped left, and to her surprise, the screen unlocked. She went to the photos first, but the folder was empty. She went to the text messages next and saw a back-and-forth exchange between Victor and someone named Monique. Q'Bita reached into the drawer and rooted around for paper and a pencil. She wanted to write down some of the names and numbers from the phone and ask Jamie to do some digging. The more she could learn about this man the closer she would be to learning why Henri had asked her to call Victor in the first place.

***

Alain crept closer to the bedroom and stopped just outside the doorway. He raised the gun and was about to make his move when he caught sight of the intruder. His heart almost exploded in his chest when he saw the woman sitting on the edge of the bed with her back to him. He knew instantly who she was, and she was holding his phone. A wave of nausea rolled over him, but he remained still and silent. He waited a split second, then lowered the gun, and was getting ready to sneak back out of the room when a small dog crawled out from under the bed and spotted him. The dog let out a bark, and in the space of few seconds everything went to hell.

Q'Bita was so wrapped up in her snooping she'd completely forgotten about Allegro until he let out a bark. She jumped up and turned in the direction of his bark. It took a second to register what she was seeing, and just about the time her brain made sense of it all, she let out a scream and everything went black.

Chapter 6

Liddy Lou Cormier was glad to be on the road, headed back to the Red Herring Inn. Her trip to Charleston had proven productive but her progress was still slower than she'd have liked. She wasn't getting any younger, and while she lived life with few regrets, she would never be able to rest peacefully for all eternity without knowing the truth about what had happened to her Henry.

Henry Cormier had been a charming and handsome man in his day. He'd swept her off her feet the first time they'd met. His blond, wavy hair sparkled like the sun, and his eyes were as deep and blue as the ocean. In a world filled with tension that threatened to boil over any second, there was a stillness to his character that she found attractive.

He'd come to her small town, along with a few others, championing the cause of civil rights. It was a tumultuous time in the South, and interracial couples were still taboo in most places. Her own family had been less than thrilled when she told them that she was in love and planned to follow Henry Cormier wherever it took her. She'd never imagined that things would end the way they did. Of course, all these years later, what haunted her the most was that she still had no idea what the truth was.

From the beginning, Henry and his friends had been on the wrong side of some very powerful people who didn't want to see the world change, and in some respects, she wasn't entirely sure the world had changed. Hate and power were still just as prevalent today as they were back then. They just manifested themselves in different ways.

She was so lost in thought that she almost missed the turn-off to the access road. She cut the wheel hard, causing the tires to squeal as she made the turn. As she looked up, she saw Andy driving right behind her. She could see him laughing and shaking his head, and she felt her face flush.

He pulled in beside her and hopped out of his SUV. She opened her own door and decided to cut him off before he started on his lecture. "Don't you start on me, Andy Hansen. I'm an old woman and I'll drive like a drunken teenager if I want to."

"Yes, Mam," Andy replied. "I was just wondering if NASCAR season had started early, is all."

"Why don't you bring some of that sass over here and help an old woman with her bags?"

Andy retrieved the bags from the back seat and helped her into the lobby. They no sooner reached the lobby when Julie rushed up to them, looking frazzled.

"Oh, thank goodness you're here, Sheriff. I just got a call from one of the guests. I'm not sure what happened but something's wrong with Q'Bita."

Liddy Lou's stomach did a flip as she watched a look of fear wash over Andy.

"Follow me. I'll take you to her."

They both followed her up the stairs and down the hall to a room on the second floor.

A familiar-looking woman greeted them at the door, but Liddy Lou couldn't place her.

"She's in here. I think she might have fainted."

Andy pushed past the woman and rushed inside. The woman smiled at Liddy Lou and said, "It's been years. I'm not surprised you don't remember."

Liddy Lou looked closer and finally realized who the woman was.

"Lizzy Collins?"

"Hello, Louie," Elizabeth said as she reached forward to hug Liddy Lou.

"Let's go check on your granddaughter. We can catch up later."

***

Q'Bita opened her eyes and was surprised to see Andy standing over her, looking concerned. Her head was swimming and she was struggling to remember something important but everyone talking at once wasn't helping. She was laying on the floor and wasn't sure how she'd gotten

25

there.

"Q'Bita, can you hear me?" Andy asked.

"Ya, I'm fine. Help me up, please."

She noticed her nana standing next to Harp Collins and his wife, and Julie from the front desk was standing behind them, wringing her hands. Someone was missing, though. She spotted Allegro and he barked at her. Then it hit her, and she shot up from the floor, almost knocking Andy over. "Where is he?"

"Who?" Andy asked.

"Alain. Victor is Alain."

"Q'Bita, not this again," Andy said quietly.

"No, Andy, I'm serious. He was here. I saw him."

Q'Bita saw a look of concern pass between Andy and her nana. She bent over and picked up Allegro and then sat on the edge of the bed.

"Honey, I'm not doubting you. I'm just not sure you're thinking clearly, that's all."

"Andy, I know what I saw, and trust me, my dead husband was standing in that doorway with a gun in his hand."

"Wait, he has a gun? Why didn't you tell me sooner?"

Andy spun towards Julie and snapped into Sheriff mode.

"We need to lock this place down now. Show me where your security footage is. I need to see where this person went when they left this room."

"Andy, calm down. I don't think Alain has any intention of using the gun. I'm in his room without his permission, going through his belongings. I'm sure he thought I was someone else and just overreacted."

"Okay, there are so many things wrong with what you just said that I don't even know where to begin, but we can discuss this later, after I find this guy."

Andy turned and followed Julie out the door, leaving Q'Bita, her nana, and the Collinses looking at each other awkwardly.

Her nana moved closer and wrapped her in a hug. "It's gonna be okay, baby girl. You just need some rest."

"Why doesn't anyone believe me? I was married to the man for seven years. I know my own husband when I see him. He's not dead. He was very much alive."

Her nana stepped back and fixed her with an appraising look. After a few seconds, she nodded at Q'Bita. "I can see that you're convinced. I have no reason to doubt you, so let's put our heads together and see what we can figure out."

Q'Bita turned to Harp and Elizabeth Collins. "I'm sorry, you must think we're crazy people around here, but I can explain."

Elizabeth looked at Harp, who bobbed his head in a gesture that implied she should speak for them both. "Trust me, darling, there's nothing you can do or say that would shock us. We've known your grandmother longer than you've been alive, and we've been through some things… to say the least."

"Oh gosh, that's right. With everything going on I completely forgot about that."

Liddy Lou wrapped an arm around Elizabeth and steered her towards the door. "I think we could all use some sweet tea and fresh air. Let's go sit on the porch and see if we can't talk this out."

***

By the time Andy and Julie reached the office, Jamie had arrived for his shift. He quickly filled Jamie in on what had happened while Jamie got to work on the security tapes.

"Tell me you have footage of this Victor guy that has Q'Bita so spooked."

"I'll see what I can do, but I can't promise anything. He managed to dodge the cameras when he arrived, and I haven't caught him on them yet. If you ask me, he's got some special skill when it comes to not being seen."

Jamie scanned through the footage from the second floor and came up empty. He was just about to give up when Andy asked to see the outside footage. A few seconds later they hit pay dirt.

"There. Stop," Andy yelled.

Jamie paused the footage and rolled it back a few frames. The camera outside the cooking school showed a black car swerve to avoid some of the chickens crossing the driveway. The car came inside the range of the camera just long enough to capture a side profile of the driver.

"Can you zoom in a little and print that out?" Andy asked.

"Do you even need to ask? I got skillz, son."

As soon as the picture hit the printer, Andy snatched it off and headed out of the office toward the front door.

"Uh, hello. Wait for me," Jamie said, chasing after him. "Where are we going?"

"To find Beecher. I need someone with a level head to look at this picture."

Andy covered the distance to the barn in record time and found Beecher inside, stacking feed.

"Hey, guys. You look serious. What's going on?"

Andy thrust the photo towards him. "Have you ever seen this guy before?"

Andy watched as Beecher's eyes went wide.

"Um, this might sound crazy, but this guy is a dead ringer for Alain. Okay, poor word choice."

"Are you sure, Beecher?" Andy asked.

"It's been a few years, but the resemblance is uncanny. I mean we both know it's not him. He's dead, so it can't be him, but it sure does look like him."

Andy rubbed his chin as he stared at the picture, trying to make sense of it all.

"Um, I hate to bring this up, but I sort of remember Q'Bita telling me once that the accident was so bad that they had to use dental records to identify the body. How hard would something like that be to fake?" Jamie asked.

Andy cocked his head in thought and then ran his hand across his face. "Not too hard at all for someone with a law-enforcement background and connections. He worked for Interpol, right?"

"Yes," Beecher and Jamie replied in unison.

"We need to find this guy and get to the bottom of this. If Q'Bita's right and he is walking around with a gun, I want to know who he really is and why he's here. If it has anything at all to do with Q'Bita, I want to know."

"How bad do you want to find him?" Jamie asked with a hint of mischief in his voice.

"Bad, and since I'm not the Castle Creek Sheriff at the moment, I don't care what laws you have to break to find him."

"I'm glad you feel that way, because he's driving a rental car and they all have GPS trackers on them. I started a search against his car while we were looking at the security footage. It should have found something by now."

Andy and Beecher followed Jamie back to the office, and all three of them crowded around Jamie's laptop.

"What the hell?" Jamie exclaimed.

"Well, don't keep us in suspense. Do you got him or not?" Beecher asked.

"I do, and you won't believe this but he's at the Sheriff's station."

Andy tugged his cell phone out of his pocket and punched at the screen. A few seconds later Mike Collins answered, and Andy cut him off immediately.

"Don't say my name. I don't want anyone to know it's me."

"Okay, but what's with the cloak and dagger?" Mike asked.

"I need you to answer my question with just a yes or a no. Did a guy named Victor Cortez just show up there?"

"Yes."

"Shit. Is he still there?"

"Yes"

"I need you to keep him there until I get there. Whatever you do, don't let him leave."

"Shouldn't be a problem."

"I mean it, Mikey; this is important. I'm on my way but keep that between us, please."

Andy hung up and started out of the office but stopped when Q'Bita appeared in the doorway.

"Are you okay?"

"I'm fine. Just wondering what I'm interrupting."

Andy looked back at Beecher and Jamie, who were both avoiding eye contact with him and suddenly had nothing to say.

"Sweetheart, I don't want to upset you, but we managed to get a picture of this guy on the security camera. I showed it to Beecher and…" Andy's voice cracked as he spoke.

"And what?" Q'Bita asked sharply.

"It's possible that you've been right all along," Andy said quietly.

"Are you saying it's Alain?"

Beecher stepped around the edge of the desk and put a hand on his sister's shoulder.

"I want to see it," Q'Bita said.

Andy felt his heart shatter in his chest as he watched Q'Bita's eyes fill with tears. She looked up at him with a helpless look and asked, "But how? It's not possible. I watched them put his body in the ground."

As Castle Creek Sheriff, Andy had dealt with countless distraught people, but this wasn't just anyone, this was the only woman he had ever loved. The woman he was planning on spending the rest of his life with. He had no idea what to tell her. He reached out and pulled her close. He could feel her shaking against him and he had to hold back his own tears. He kissed the top of her head and whispered, "I love you and I promise you, I will get to the bottom of this."

Chapter 7

Alain paced back and forth in what he assumed had been Andy Hansen's office at one time. He was only half-listening as the acting sheriff droned on about what had happened leading up to Gianni Marini's arrest. Alain already knew most of the details and didn't need the armchair quarterback version, but he needed to win over this feckless redneck if he had any hope of convincing him to turn Marini over to him.

Alain stopped in front of a wall of pictures and examined several featuring Andy Hansen. He scowled at how the montage depicted Hansen as the clichéd all-American good guy, then noticed that Chance had stopped talking. Alain glanced over his shoulder and was surprised to see the smirk on Chance's face.

"That's Andy Hansen. He was the Castle Creek Sheriff before they upgraded to me."

"That sounds like an interesting story. Are you free to share the details?" Alain asked.

He listened for a few minutes but quickly lost all interest and decided that this current sheriff was so full of hot air he could power his own balloon and keep it afloat in a tornado.

"Are you still with me?" Chance asked.

"Um, yes, I believe so. It's a riveting story to say the least. You're quite the hero, for sure. It's obvious that your predecessor was a rule breaker and a disgrace to the badge. The village was right to choose you as his replacement."

"Village? Castle Creek may be small and rural but we're definitely not a village," Chance said defensively.

The both looked up as the office door opened and a deputy appeared in the doorway.

"Not now, Mikey, we're busy here," Chance snapped.

"Sorry but I need to speak to you about something urgent."

"Unless it involves fire, zombies, or plagues of locusts, it can wait."

"Ya, it's something like that. Can you come out here?" Mike asked with some urgency.

"What part of I don't care did you have trouble with, Mikey?"

Alain saw a huge presence push its way past the deputy and enter the office.

"Sorry, Mikey, I don't have time for Chance's bullshit right now."

Alain felt a wave of panic wash over him as Andy Hansen stopped in front of him and fixed him with a less than welcoming stare.

"You can't just come barging in here like you own the place, Hansen. This is my rodeo now, and I call the shots."

"Shut up, Chance. Victor and I need to have a chat and I'm not leaving until we do."

Chance was about to lay into Andy again when Alain started for the door. "I'll let you two go on with your posturing and chest-thumping while I retrieve my prisoner and get out of your hair."

He made it about two more steps before Andy moved to block his path. "You're not going anywhere until I get to the bottom of who the hell you really are."

"He's with Interpol, you jackass, so get your hands off him before you end up in the cell with Marini. On second thought, keep going. Marini ordered you killed. Maybe he'll finish the job himself if I lock you up with him."

"I wouldn't joke about such things, Sheriff. Gianni Marini is a very dangerous man, which is why it would be in everyone's best interest to turn him over to my custody so I can take him back to France," Alain said.

"No one is turning anyone over to you, and you aren't going anywhere until I get some answers," Andy growled.

"Very well. What is it you need from me, Mr. Hansen?"

"Let's start with why my fiancée seems to think you're her dead husband."

Alain took a step back and felt the temperature increase tenfold in the room. This was not how he'd pictured any of this playing out.

***

Q'Bita sat quietly, listening to the others chit-chat and catch up on all the years that had passed since they were last together. From the little bits that sank in, Q'Bita gathered that Harp and Elizabeth had been close with her grandparents but had fallen out of touch after her grandfather's death. They also seemed to carry some degree of guilt about it, but her nana insisted that apologies weren't necessary between old friends.

Jamie reached out and touched her arm, and Q'Bita jumped. She'd completely forgotten he was there. He handed Allegro to her. The small dog licked her chin then made a circle in her lap before settling in for a nap. She yawned as the urge to join him washed over her.

"Q'B-Doll, why don't you go take a nap? I'll wake you as soon as Andy gets back."

"Thanks, Jamie, but I'm afraid if I tried to sleep, I'd just have nightmares. Hopefully, Andy will get to the bottom of this soon and we can put it all behind us."

The others had all stopped talking and were now looking at her, but she wasn't sure what to say.

"I feel like all I've done since you arrived is apologize to you for the craziness. I swear it's normally not like this at all around here."

Her nana laughed. "Child, you have no idea some of the adventures these two have been involved in. There's nothing happening here that would even surprise them."

A snorting sound from the steps announced Rene's arrival. He immediately launched into one of his pseudo-indignant hissy fits.

"So resurrected exes are just an everyday occurrence now and no one feels the need to loop me in? I'd hate to see what you people call a catastrophe. Would summoning Satan and inviting him to high tea qualify as a reason to at least send me a text or a tweet?"

Rene sauntered up the steps and stopped in front of the table. He poured himself a glass of iced tea and snagged a few cookies before turning towards Q'Bita. "So are you all just going to sit there admiring my exquisite sense of fashion or is someone going to fill me in? I'm missing my afternoon beauty nap to comfort you. The least you could do is give me some details."

"I don't have any details to give you that you probably haven't already heard from Beecher. The man staying here under the name Victor Cortez looks and sounds very much like Alain. Andy is at the station now, trying to get this all sorted out."

"OMG, maybe Alain had a secret twin or was some kind of pod person. What if he's a clone? Oh, that would be so weird. I mean, are they exact copies or do they have little quirky differences? Kind of like those undies you had as a kid where each pair looked exactly the same but had a different day of the week stamped on the front."

Q'Bita was about to put the brakes on her brother-in-law's oral regurgitation when Andy's SUV appeared in the driveway. She could see that he was talking on the phone. His call lasted a few more minutes and then he stepped out of the truck. The look on his face was a cross between anger and confusion as he made his way towards them.

Before she even got a chance to speak, Rene jumped on Andy. "Well, is it Alain or not? We've been waiting here forever and you're just standing there like someone snatched out your tongue."

Q'Bita could see Andy trying to choose his words carefully, and she wasn't sure he was going to be able to pull it off but he surprised her.

"Rene, I'm sure everyone would like to know what's going on but I think it's better if I discuss this with Q'Bita first, and she can decide what she wants to share later."

Rene looked mortally wounded but Q'Bita was sure he'd recover. His penchant for the dramatic had an elasticity that an Olympic gymnast would envy. She scooped up Allegro and stood up. "Maybe it would be better if we went inside to finish this conversation."

Andy reached out and took Allegro then followed her inside to the cooking school.

"Sit. I'll get you some pie and then we can talk."

"Q'Bita, forget the pie. It can wait."

Q'Bita felt her lower lip trembling. The pie had been her way of putting off their conversation but Andy had obviously seen right through her. She also knew that Andy Hansen turning down pie was probably how the apocalypse would start.

She sat down across from him but kept her eyes fixed on her hands. She could feel his eyes on her and she knew if she looked up, she would break.

Andy reached one massive hand across the counter and wrapped it around both of hers. "First, I want to say that I'm sorry. I haven't handled any of this the way I should have. I can't explain it but every time I hear his name something inside me goes on the defensive. When you said his name that night in the hospital it was like a punch to the liver. I guess there's a part of me that wishes he never existed. It's selfish and I need to get past it."

Q'Bita wanted to stop him but she couldn't form a single word. As much as she wanted to know the truth, she also knew that once she did, things would never be the same. She loved her quiet, mostly uneventful life here in Castle Creek with Andy and her family, and the thought of that changing made her sick.

Andy had just started talking again when someone knocked on the side door. The sound startled Allegro and he started barking. Q'Bita walked to the door, pulled it open, then froze. Standing on the other side was the last person she had expected to see at this moment.

"Q'Bita, I don't know what he's told you, but I can explain."

Chapter 8

Q'Bita could see Alain's mouth moving but had no idea what he'd said after, "I can explain." All she heard was the buzzing of her blood pressure rising dangerously high. It felt like she was watching a movie in slow motion. One minute she was standing still, staring at a ghost, and the next she lost all semblance of self-control and punched him in the face.

A look of shock registered on Alain's face as a rivulet of blood trickled from his nose. Andy was now at her side, and he looked almost as surprised as Alain.

"You can explain? I seriously doubt there's anything you can say right now that would adequately explain to me how, or why, you're standing here in front of me. In case you've forgotten, the last time I saw you, you were supposedly in a coffin being lowered into the ground. People don't usually come back from something like that."

"Q'Bita, I understand how shocking this is for you but I think you broke my nose. Can I please have some ice and a towel?"

His reply did nothing to calm her anger, and she lunged for him like Rolfie going after a bird in the garden. Andy wrapped one big arm around her waist and pulled her back as Alain scrambled backwards against the doorframe.

"Okay, slugger, take it easy. I think you have him on the ropes," Andy chuckled.

Andy sat her down then positioned himself between her and Alain. "I'm going to go to the walk-in and grab some ice. You two think you can stay in your own corners until I get back?"

Q'Bita crossed her arms over her chest and glared at Alain, who was still holding one hand to his bleeding nose. She reached behind her, grabbed a stack of napkins from the counter, and tossed them toward him. They fluttered to the ground a few inches from Alain but he stayed glued to the wall until Andy returned.

She watched as Andy handed Alain a bag of frozen carrots.

"I thought you were getting me ice," Alain snarked.

"Couldn't find any. They're frozen. Take it or leave it. I couldn't care less."

"I didn't expect to be welcomed with open arms but is it too much to ask for a modicum of courtesy?"

"I didn't expect you to come back from the dead, so yes, you are asking too much," Q'Bita said tersely.

"As I said, I can explain, but I'd prefer to do so in private, provided you can control your temper long enough to hear me out."

Q'Bita looked at Andy, who shrugged and said, "It's up to you, babe. I'll go if you want, or stay if you want."

"Go, I guess, but don't go too far. Depending on what comes out of his mouth next, I'm not sure I trust myself."

Q'Bita waited for Andy to leave, then pulled out a stool, and motioned for Alain to take a seat. She contemplated kicking it out from under him as he sat down but managed to control herself. Alain remained quiet. He was staring at her and she was beginning to feel uncomfortable.

"Well?" she asked.

"It's good to see you, Q'Bita. Except for the broken nose part."

"Seriously? Were you this much of an ass when we were married?"

"Okay, I get that you're upset. Obviously, I'm not dead, and I know you'll find this hard to believe, but I did this for you."

"So let me get this straight. You faked your death and left me devastated because you thought I'd appreciate it?"

"No, of course not. I did this for your safety. I..."

His voice trailed off mid-sentence, and she could see that he was struggling to find the right words to say whatever it was he wanted to say. She chided herself for enjoying his discomfort but then found herself getting angry with him all over again when he stopped struggling and started staring at her again like some lovesick puppy dog.

"I'm waiting," Q'Bita said impatiently.

"Okay, I'll tell you everything but you have to promise you're not going to punch me again." Q'Bita rolled her eyes and wrinkled her nose in disgust but kept her comments to herself.

"While we were married, you may have been under the impression that I was an analyst for Interpol. In hind sight, I should have been slightly more forthcoming with you."

Alain paused again and waited for her to say something.

"Oh, by all means, please go on. I'd hate to interrupt you while you're trying to explain to me how our whole marriage appears to have been built on a lie. I'm riveted and can't imagine what's coming next."

"I'm actually an agent with Interpol, not an analyst. I work undercover, dealing with international smuggling rings. Shortly after we married, I made an enemy of a very connected and dangerous man. It took a while for him to track down my real identity, but a few months before my accident my cover was made and this man put a price on my head. He wouldn't have been content to just kill me, he would have made sure that you were part of the bargain, and I couldn't allow that. Faking my death was the only way to protect you."

Q'Bita sat quietly, stunned by what she'd just heard. She wasn't sure what she thought his excuse was going to be but it sure wasn't what he'd just shared.

"I understand that this is a lot to process, but I need you to know that if there had been any other way, I would not have done this. When Henri told me that you'd gone and gotten engaged I knew that I needed to let you know the truth. I love you just as much now as I did then, and I'm committed to doing whatever it takes to make this right between us. I can't let you make such a big mistake. I'm your husband and we belong together."

Q'Bita was about to punch him again when the swinging door to the dining room flew open and Andy burst in, looking like a man possessed. He covered the distance between the door and Alain in two large steps.

"Who the hell do you think you are? You can't come waltzing back in here and think that I'm going to just step aside and let you back into Q'Bita's life like none of this ever happened. Her heart isn't a revolving door, you ass, and I won't let you hurt her again."

Alain scurried backwards off the stool, putting a few feet between himself and Andy.

"I think I know my own wife, and in case you haven't figured this out by now, she isn't the type to let some inbred piece of meat tell her what to do. If I were you, I'd—"

"Shut up! Both of you," Q'Bita screeched.

They both turned and looked at her like she'd just fired off a round from a shotgun in church.

"Andy, I appreciate that you love me and want to protect me but I assure you, under no circumstances is this man going to get back in my good graces any time within this century."

She turned to face Alain. "Apparently you don't know me as well as you think you do. While you may have survived your fake death, our marriage did not. It died the second you made the decision to do something so unforgivable. I've moved on and I love Andy. He is the man I plan to spend the rest of my life with, and you can just go back to wherever you came from and forget that I ever existed."

Andy took two more steps and pushed open the door to the driveway. "I'm not going to hold this door open much longer. If I were you, I'd take this opportunity to leave on your own before I change my mind and decide to help you leave."

Alain took a tentative step toward Q'Bita and then turned toward Andy. "With all due respect, this is between me and my wife."

"Will you please stop calling me your wife? Our marriage ended with your supposed death."

A look of smug self-satisfaction crossed Alain's face, and Q'Bita felt her stomach churn.

"Actually, Q'Bita, you're wrong about that. I'm very good at what I do. The death certificate, insurance payout, and other small details were all my doing. None of it was real. My contacts within Interpol assisted with the legal details, so as far as the authorities are concerned, I am still very much alive, and still your husband."

Andy let the screen door thump shut. "Okay, smart guy, why go to all that trouble and then come here and risk being found out? Doesn't seem like a very smart plan to me."

"You have your own incompetence to thank for that. If your department hadn't messed up so badly with Gianni Marini, not to mention almost getting Henri killed in the process, I would have stayed safely hidden away in Lyon."

Q'Bita didn't have to guess what was going to happen next if she didn't put a stop to this now. She knew Andy well enough to know that Alain had just crossed a line from which there was no coming back. She lunged forward and planted herself directly between them.

"Okay, I've heard enough. Alain, I don't care what your reasons or excuses are, we're done here. It's getting late, and I doubt there are any other rooms available due to the festival, so you can stay for the evening, but you need to be gone before check-out tomorrow."

Alain looked agitated but she really didn't care.

"I'd forgotten how stubborn you can be at times. I have work to attend to so I'll go for now, but I'm hoping that once you've had time to process this further, you'll come to your senses and we can continue this discussion."

Alain tossed the half-thawed carrots and bloody towel into the sink then walked out of the kitchen without waiting for a reply.

Q'Bita watched the dining room door swinging back and forth for a few seconds then turned to Andy. His expression was a mixture of anger and confusion. She knew she should say something but words failed her.

Andy's voice cracked as he spoke, "Are you okay?"

Q'Bita bit down hard on her lower lip and nodded her head. She knew if she tried to talk, she'd just end up dissolving into a river of tears. Andy came closer and she could see his hands shaking. She reached out, grabbed one of his meat paws with her tiny hand, pulled it to her lips, and gave it a kiss.

Andy returned the gesture by stroking her check and then pulled her into his chest and held her tight.

"Go ahead. Smell me. I know how much you like it," he said with a chuckle.

"Andy Hansen, I have never loved you as much as I do right this minute."

Chapter 9

Q'Bita hadn't slept well and needed a pick-me-up. The kitchen was just the place to make that happen. She had just pulled her famous double-layer Cherry Chocolate Crunch cake out of the oven and the room was bathed in the intoxicating aroma of warm chocolate and the sweet scent of succulent cherries. She placed the steaming, dark layers on the cooling racks and had just closed the oven door when the sound of a commotion moving quickly towards the kitchen caught her attention.

The door to the kitchen exploded inward as her brother-in-law, Rene, made his entrance. One look at his disheveled appearance and panicked expression told her something wasn't quite right. Flamboyant was an understatement when used to describe her brother Beecher's husband. Rene was the human equivalent of putting a new battery in a vibrating toothbrush, and he seemed to be in an epic swirl today.

"Q'Bita, come quick. Beecher's lost it and he's halfway to Put's place with a loaded rifle." Without any further explanation, all six-foot-three, two hundred and fifty pounds of Rene pirouetted with the grace of a prima ballerina and sprinted towards the side door that lead to the parking lot.

He paused in the doorway and then screeched, "Q'Bita, don't just stand there with your mouth open. Light a fire under it, sister, or get your checkbook ready, because Beecher was in a full-blown hissy, and if you don't get over to the Newsomes' place and talk him down, he is going to need bail money and a lawyer."

Q'Bita followed Rene out the door, past the herb garden, and across the gravel drive. As they reached Rene's car, Q'Bita barely had time to take in the damage to the passenger side when a shot rang out from the direction of the Newsomes' farm.

Rene blanched. "Oh, Lord love a duck, please let that have been a car backfiring and not the start of my husband's murder trial."

The pair hopped into Rene's once-beautiful Alfa Romeo convertible and careened across the access road separating the Red Herring Inn and the Newsomes' farm. When they reached the farm, Rene slammed on the brakes and slid to a stop.

Q'Bita gasped as she took in the almost comical standoff taking place. A scarlet-faced Beecher was just lowering the rifle he'd been pointing at a ghost-white Put, and eighty-something, fragile-as-fine-porcelain Evie was pointing the biggest double-barreled, over/under shotgun Q'Bita had ever seen directly at Beecher.

Since her recent diagnosis of essential tremors, Evie Newsome could hardly open a pickle jar on her own when she taught her monthly canning classes at the Red Herring cooking school but she held that shot gun like an outlaw biker robbing a liquor store—not so much as a wiggle, let alone the tremors that occasionally robbed her of her dexterity.

Rene and Q'Bita jumped out of the car and started towards the standoff. Put spit a mouthful of Skol juice towards Beecher's feet and made one of his frequent and uncalled-for comments meant to belittle Beecher and Rene. "Well, lookie here. Captain Rainbow has come to save you, and he brought backup. At least my wife brought a shotgun."

Beecher made a low growling noise and lunged towards Put, but Evie raised the big old double-barreled shotgun towards the sky and let loose the second round. Everyone froze.

Evie looked at Q'Bita and calmly said, "Q'Bita, would you kindly disarm your brother and remove him from my property? I'm going to take my ass of a husband to task for running poor Rene off the road and there may be language involved that's best used by a lady in private. When he's been put in his place, I'll come by and we can work out the details of getting Rene's automobile fixed."

Beecher started to protest but Rene interrupted him. "Beecher, please, let's just go. I'm not hurt, the car can be fixed, and if she reloads and lets off another shot, I just might soil myself."

Beecher reluctantly moved away from Put and started towards his truck but Put just couldn't resist getting in one more taunt. "I don't see what the big issue is. So I bumped his little go-cart off the road. I thought you fairies could fly."

Beecher rounded on Put and raised his rifle again but Q'Bita quickly countered his move by stepping in between them. "Beecher, calm down.

Put may be a bigot and a fool but he is not worth a life sentence." Beecher was so furious he was shaking, and Q'Bita could see tears welling in his eyes. She hadn't seen him this angry since they were teenagers, and it scared her.

Beecher took a deep breath and glanced towards Rene. From where Q'Bita stood, he appeared about to faint. Q'Bita let out her breath as Beecher turned back towards her and lowered the gun, but the wild look that frightened Q'Bita was still very much present.

"Hear me loud and clear, you old prick. One of these days that hateful mouth of yours is going to be your undoing, and if you ever try to hurt my husband again, I will see to it personally that Miss Evie is eating condolence casserole for a month."

Evie winked at Q'Bita then glared at her husband. "Putnam Everett Newsome, you cantankerous old goat, get your arse in the house before you make me a widow and cheat the good Lord out of his right to call you home or send you south for your sins."

Q'Bita placed an arm around Beecher's shoulders and gently guided him to his truck. "Rene, I think I'll ride back with Beecher and keep him out of trouble. We'll see you at home."

Beecher didn't say anything on the drive back to the Red Herring Inn. They pulled into the main drive, and Q'Bita was about to say something when Beecher turned to her.

"Q'Bita, I know you're concerned but the last damn thing I need right now is a lecture. That old fool is so full of hate that we both know I would be doing the world a favor if I put him down. He could have killed Rene, running him into the ditch like that. I get that he doesn't approve of my lifestyle but I will protect my family no matter what the cost."

Q'Bita could tell her brother was still angry, so she chose her words carefully. "Beecher, I love you, and you know that this family loves Rene, but there are always going to be people in this world who cannot accept your right to live your life as you choose. Those people's opinions cannot be changed but your reaction to them gives them power over you that they don't deserve. When it comes to the Put Newsomes of the world, you cannot let their narrowmindedness ruin the life you've built for yourself and Rene. You are a good person and you deserve happiness."

Beecher finally relaxed and let out a little sigh. He racked the rifle in its holder on the back window of the truck and opened the door. He gave

Q'Bita a weak smile as he closed the door and grabbed the crossbow he'd been hunting with earlier that day from the bed of the truck. He walked off towards Rene, who was making a show of fussing over the damage to his car while pretending not to be eavesdropping on Beecher and Q'Bita's conversation.

Q'Bita got out of the truck and Rene mouthed a silent thank you to her as she headed back to the kitchen to check on her cake.

Chapter 10

Andy paced back and forth like a caged animal waiting for the door to his former office to open. Mike Collins had just asked him for the third time if he wanted a cup of coffee and it was starting to annoy him.

"Mikey, I know you're just trying to be polite but do I look like a man who needs more caffeine?"

"Sorry, boss, I know this must suck. I'm trying to take your mind off it, that's all."

The fact that Mikey still called him boss should have been a comfort, but instead it just reinforced the fact that he was in the bullpen, pacing, while Chance and Alain were inside Andy's office discussing what was going to happen with Gianni Marini.

The sound of boots coming toward him caused Andy to turn around. He cussed under his breath at the sight of Red Dixon.

"What are you doing here, Hansen? This ain't your chicken coop anymore."

Andy choked back the first reply that came to his mind and decided to just go with, "I'm here to make sure Chance doesn't do anything stupid."

Red laughed and then spit a wad of chew into a nearby garbage can.

"Jesus, Red, have some class. This is county property, not your back yard."

Andy felt his stomach turn as a huge crap-eating smile spread across Red's face.

"I guess you haven't heard the good news. I'm surprised your boy Mikey didn't tell you, Hansen."

"Quit trying to bait me and just tell me what horseshit you're up to now."

"In light of all the recent unfortunate events, I thought I'd save the county some money and offer up my security force as an alternative law enforcement option. The initial conversations with the Mayor and the County Commissioners have been quite productive. With any luck, I'll have a decision in a few weeks."

Andy could feel himself getting angry, and he tried to count backwards from 100, but only made it to 92 before he exploded. "You have got to be shitting me. Do you really think that I'm just going to roll over and let you steal my department out from underneath me? If you do, then you're an even bigger jack hole than Chance."

Andy had been so fired up that he hadn't heard the door open behind him.

"That's Sheriff Jack Hole to you, Hansen, and you'd better get a handle on your temper and pipe the hell down before I slap you with a disturbing-the-peace charge."

"Kiss my ass, Chance. You don't scare me."

"Gentlemen. If you don't mind, I'd like to process Mr. Marini now and be on my way."

Andy looked past Chance and saw Alain standing in the doorway. He looked bored, and it pissed Andy off even more.

"What does he mean, process Marini? Marini tried to have me killed, and he's a material witness in my grandfather's case. He isn't going anywhere."

"Hate to break it to you, Andy, but you've got no skin in this game. Frenchie here is Interpol, and I ain't about to make an enemy of those fellas. Marini only suggested that his guy kill you, but you're alive and well, and I have Jock's killer, so as far as I'm concerned there's no reason to keep Marini in custody."

"Have you lost your freaking mind, Chance? Marini is a dangerous criminal, and you don't have any idea what this one has done," Andy said, motioning to Alain. "Did he even bother to tell you that his real name isn't Victor Cortez?"

"Actually, Andrew, I've been completely forthcoming with Sheriff Holleran, and he's well aware that Gianni Marini is the key to me locating my enemy. I would have thought you of all people would be supportive, considering my enemy wouldn't hesitate to come after my wife, and we all know how fond of her you are."

Andy took a few steps toward Alain, fully intending to clock his smug ass, but Chance pulled out a Taser and held it up for Andy to see he meant business. "Keep coming, Andy. I'd love to fill you full of juice and watch you flop around on the floor like a carp until you piss yourself."

Andy stopped and tried to pull himself together but it was mostly a lost cause. He turned back toward Red and then growled, "This has your stink all over it, and I'm going to make sure you live to regret this, Red. One of these days you're going to need my help, and you'll wish you'd hitched your saddle to a different horse."

Chapter 11

The sky was black and heavy with storm clouds when Cane Jessop reached the Newsomes' farm. He could see his uncle Put out in the back field on the ancient, red Farmall tractor and wondered if he should go convince him to come in before the storm hit. While Cane contemplated the approaching storm, his aunt Evie appeared at the door of the farmhouse and called out for him to come inside.

Cane entered the warm kitchen and greeted Evie with a bear hug, lifting her off the ground and spinning her in circles until she scolded him. "Boy, put me down before my lunch ends up all over you. I don't want to have to strip you down to your skivvies and scrub you with a horse brush."

Cane gently placed his favorite aunt down on the faded linoleum floor and inhaled the heavenly smell of baking bread. "Smells good in here, Aunt Evie. Hope I'm invited to stay for dinner."

Evie Newsome was famous for her home-style cooking and her quilting. A mild case of essential tremors had recently kept her from doing both of the things she loved so she made the most of the shake-free days when she could. Cane could see she'd been baking up a storm to match the one just starting to rage outside.

Cane eyed up the pan of apple crisp cooling on the counter and was just about to open the oven door for a whiff of freshly baked bread when she swatted at him with a rolled-up kitchen towel.

"Cane Jessop, do not open that oven door. You'll let out all my steam and ruin the crust on the bread. Go wrangle your fool of an uncle off that tractor and get him in the barn before the good Lord sends a well-directed bolt to strike him down. Lord knows, he's certainly asked for it this week."

Cane chuckled and rubbed his stinging knuckles. "So, rumor has it that Uncle Put had quite the run-in with Beecher Block earlier. Care to elaborate on the finer details?"

Evie wagged her finger at her nephew and made a sucking noise through her teeth. "The patrons of that heathen establishment you find it necessary to frequent would do well to mind their own business but, in this case, they're correct. Your uncle got another call from those EPA fellas and was all fired up. He had the poor sense to vent his frustration by running Rene into a ditch. Beecher didn't take kindly to this and showed up here spitting fire and brandishing a rifle. Your uncle was feeling cocky because I had the drop on Beecher so he just kept running his trap and making it worse. Thank goodness Rene brought Q'Bita to fetch Beecher. Beecher still looked angry as a mud hen when they left out of here and threatened to kill your uncle if he came near Rene again. Truth be told, I have half a mind to let him, but I'd miss that old possum if anything ever happened to him."

Cane seriously doubted that his Uncle Put would ever right himself with alternative lifestyles any more than he'd right himself with sustainable, environmentally friendly farming methods. Put's orneriness had managed to get him in deep manure with both the Blocks and the EPA but there was no sense trying to reason with his uncle. Cane just hoped Evie's trusty over/under shotgun and amazing apple crisp could keep Put from getting himself in more trouble than he could handle.

Cane's self-reflection was broken by a huge clap of thunder that rattled the farmhouse windows and shook it to its foundation. Evie crossed the kitchen to the window over the sink and craned her neck, trying to catch a glimpse of Put, but she couldn't see a thing because sheets of rain were now being driven into the window screen by the wind, blocking out all view of what lay beyond.

"Cane, please go fetch that old fool before he is soaked to the bone and gets blown off that tractor."

Cane was halfway out the door when Evie called him back. "Here, boy, put on Put's coat and hat before you catch your death and your mama never forgives me for sending her baby to an early grave."

The wind was really kicking up, and Cane struggled against it. The rain stung where it hit exposed skin. He pulled up the collar of the borrowed jacket and picked up the pace. As he passed by the main barn, he noticed that Put had left the loft doors unlatched and they were being banged around by the wind. The large ladder they used to access the loft from outside the barn had fallen over and was now blocking the front doors to the barn. He knew if he did not get up there and latch those doors, he would be spending the next few days removing wet hay and laying in replacement hay. He could hear the old Farmall tractor making its way towards the barn so he made a run for the main doors and the inviting dryness that waited inside.

The old ladder to the loft creaked as he made his way up, and Cane sighed as he realized just how much work the old farm really needed. It needed a lot of TLC but his uncle was too proud and too stubborn to admit it.

Cane had just finished latching the loft doors when he heard the tractor sputtering as it pulled into the barn. He walked over to the edge of the loft and called down, "That thing's sounding as ornery as you, Uncle Put. I can probably fix the tractor. You, on the other hand—that's a big job."

His uncle gave him a scowl that reminded Cane of a scarecrow they used to have.

"What are you standing up there grinning at, boy? Get your hairy arse down here and help me button up this barn before I come up there and toss you down."

Cane chuckled, stepped onto the ladder, and started down. He was only two rungs from the top when he heard the sound of cracking wood and felt the rung give way under his foot. His boot slammed into the next rung and that one also snapped under his weight. He reached up frantically, trying to wrap his arm around the top rung, but it was too late. He landed with a thud that knocked the wind out of him.

He lay still for a second, trying to determine if anything other than the ladder was broken. His ankle throbbed but otherwise everything else seemed intact. He opened his eyes and saw his uncle standing over him with a look of concern. "Oh good, you're alive. I wasn't sure how I was going to explain this to your mama. She's gets too emotional when it comes to you."

"Really, Uncle Put?"

"Don't go getting your G-string in a knot. You're still breathing and still talking, which means you'll survive. Might have bruised your arse, but it was already cracked so no worries there."

Cane got up, dusted himself off, and walked over to the ladder. He tested the lower rungs and they all seemed fine, so he climbed up a few until he was eye level with the rungs that had broken.

"Uncle Put, did you notice anything weird with this ladder when you went up in the loft today?"

"Boy, that fall must have scrambled your brain like my morning eggs. You know darn well that your Aunt Evie declared that loft off limits for me. She says I'm getting too old to be going up and down that ladder. Guess we'd better not tell her about you little tumble or she'll declare it off limits for you too."

"Wait, are you saying you weren't up here today?"

"Dang, boy, did that fall bust your eardrums? No, I wasn't up there today. I haven't been anywhere near that loft in months. That's your job now, and in case you ain't figured it out yet, fixing my ladder is also gonna fall under your job, too."

"Okay. If you weren't up here today, then how did the doors get open? I know for certain that I latched them from the inside two days ago."

Cane looked down at his uncle and saw the look of genuine confusion on his face.

"Boy, I got no idea what you're on about."

Cane explained to his uncle about the toppled ladder blocking the front doors and the open loft doors. His uncle insisted that he had absolutely no idea how that had happened, and that there had been no toppled ladder or open doors when he'd left the barn for the field.

Cane took a closer look at one of the broken rungs. He pushed the pieces back together and felt along the back. His hand caught on what felt like a smooth incision. He did the same for the other rung and again felt the same smooth incision.

"What are you messing with, boy?"

"I know this sound crazy, but I swear someone or something cut partway through these rungs. Were you doing anything near here that might have cause this?"

"No. I've been plowing for the last few days. I ain't been hanging out in here wasting time."

Cane carefully climbed down the ladder and squatted near the ground. He could see a small pile of fine wood shavings just behind the ladder. His uncle bent down and let out a low whistle.

"Well, I'll be damned. Looks like you might be right."

Cane stood up and dusted his hands off on his jeans.

"Let's keep this between us for now. I'm gonna called Andy Hansen and have him come take a look and see what he thinks."

"Hansen? Why call him? He ain't the law around here no more. If someone's been messing with this barn you need to call Chance Holleran. Besides, if someone's trying to kill me, it's probably that fruit loop brother of Hansen's girlfriend."

Cane sighed and wondered if it was worth his breath to even go down this path with his uncle.

"Uncle Put, his name is Beecher, not fruit loop, fairy boy, or twinkle toes. I know you're not a fan of his lifestyle but he is one of my closest friends and I really wish you could just live and let live when it comes to Beecher and Rene. I'm not asking you to be buddies, I'm just asking you to be civil. Which, by the way, means you don't run Rene off the road into a ditch when you're angry."

Cane watched as his uncle hung his head and kicked at the barn floor with the toe of his boot.

"Oh, you heard about that, then, I guess. Probably wasn't my best moment."

"You think? Aunt Evie said you were mad about a call from the EPA. What did the EPA folks say that had you so riled up anyhow?"

"It wasn't the EPA, it was those lawyers they hired. They're still harping on that fella's suicide. They tried to tell me that I might be partly to blame and that I needed to cooperate or they'd make sure that fella's family extended their suit to me too."

"That's ridiculous. They can't do that. That man was supposed to come here and make sure that the farming practices in this area weren't contributing to the watershed damage. He wasn't supposed to take bribes from half the farmers in the county and turn a blind eye. You did the right thing turning him in. If he couldn't live with what he did, then that's between him and the Lord. You're not to blame."

"I know that, Cane, but those lawyers sure made it sound like I'd done something wrong, and that just pisses me off."

"I guess it would piss me off, too, but you can't take that out on other people."

His uncle looked down at the ground again and kept quiet. Cane didn't have the heart to push the subject any further.

"Why don't you go get washed up for dinner and I'll close up the barn? I'll call Andy and ask him to stop by after dinner. There's no point involving the authorities until we figure out if this was really someone else's doing or just a weird accident."

Cane watched as his uncle made his way toward the farm house. Once he was sure his uncle was not coming back, he turned his attention to the ladder. He walked to the backside of the ladder and looked up at the broken rungs. He pulled out his cell phone and turned on the flashlight app, pointed the light toward one of the broken rungs and saw something shiny reflecting the light back towards him. Cane couldn't be completely sure but he'd bet his next paycheck that he was looking at a broken saw tooth.

He closed the flashlight app then called Andy Hansen.

Chapter 12

Andy was still pissing fire by the time he'd arrived back at the Red Herring Inn. Q'Bita had seldom seen him this angry. She sat quietly and let him polish off half a vinegar pie before she worked up the courage to say anything.

"Wanna tell me what's got you so angry?"

Andy looked up from his pie and locked eyes with her. She could see his nostrils flaring and she wasn't sure if she should have asked. She waited while he took another huge bite of pie.

"That depends on whether or not you got more pie in the walk-in. It's definitely a two-pie kind of story."

Q'Bita relaxed a little and smiled at him. "Why don't you keep working on that one and I'll go see what I can find? I think I just might have a caramel apple pie hidden back there. I can pop it in the warmer and heat it up. How's that sound?"

"Sounds like I'm marrying the perfect woman."

That comment should have melted her heart and filled her with joy but instead it made her want to cry. Andy had been so focused on protecting her that she wasn't sure if he'd yet realized just how complicated things were now that Alain had returned. If Alain was telling the truth, it meant that he and Q'Bita were still legally married, which definitely put their wedding plans on hold.

She popped the pie into the warmer and returned to table. She listened as Andy told her everything that had happened at the station. By the time he was finished, he'd polished off the whole vinegar pie and half the caramel apple pie.

"Should I wrap this up and take it upstairs with us?" Q'Bita asked jokingly.

Andy rubbed his stomach and let out a small belch. "Ya. Sooner or later Alain is going to show up here and I'll need something to distract me."

"If Chance really is stupid enough to release Gianni Marini to Alain, will he be coming back here too?"

"No, it will take a while for all the necessary paperwork and transport arrangements. Marini will stay in lock-up until all that's done. He'll most likely stay there until they fly back to France."

Q'Bita was listening to Andy but she was also thinking about how little time she might have left with Allegro, and it broke her heart. She'd become so attached to the puppy that she couldn't bear to say goodbye.

"So, is that look of sadness on your face about the dog or Alain?"

Q'Bita was about to get defensive when she noticed the smirk on Andy's face.

"Definitely Allegro. I promise."

"I'm sorry. I know you're attached to the little guy but he was never ours to keep, Q'Bita."

Q'Bita was about to question Andy choice of the word 'ours' when his phone rang. Andy looked down at the display and then held up a finger. She listened to Andy's side of the conversation and gathered that someone needed him. He sighed as he hung up.

"Any chance you can put the rest of that pie, and our conversation, on hold for a while? Something's going on next door and Cane needs me to stop over."

"Stop over as a friend or as a cop?" Q'Bita asked.

"A little of both. Sounds like someone may have been messing with Put's barn. Probably just kids but it can't hurt to head over and check it out."

Q'Bita walked him to the door and gave him a quick kiss. "Be safe. The pie will be waiting for you when you get back."

"Just the pie?" Andy asked with a devilish chuckle.

Q'Bita gave him a slap on the arm and a small dismissive wave then returned to the kitchen to wrap up the pie. She was almost finished when the door from the dining room swung inward and Alain entered the kitchen.

"Good, you're alone."

Q'Bita stopped what she was doing and stared him down. "I thought I made myself clear, Alain. What part of pack your crap and leave didn't you understand?"

Alain smiled in an attempt to defuse her anger. "I heard you loud and clear but I think you might want to hear me out before you toss me to the wolves."

"The only thing I want to hear is the sound of your rental car leaving for the airport."

"Is that so? What if I told you it was about Allegro?"

"I already heard that you're taking Gianni Marini back with you and I realize that means Allegro as well. I'll gather his things and have Jamie bring him to you when you're ready to check out."

Q'Bita tried to choke back the tears as they stung her eyes.

"That won't be necessary."

"What do you mean?"

"I understand that you're angry with me but there has to be a part of you that still remembers the man you married. Have I ever denied you anything your heart desired?"

Q'Bita planted her hands on her hips and stared at him warily. "Quit playing games and just tell me what's going on, Alain."

"I know how attached you are to Allegro so I've made certain accommodations with Gianni in exchange for him allowing you to keep Allegro."

For a split second Q'Bita forgot how angry she was with her ex and almost wrapped him in a huge hug but got herself under control quickly.

"This is unexpected. I don't know what to say."

Alain beamed like he'd just won the lottery. "I'm glad you're pleased. I was hoping you'd take this gesture as a peace offering and consider letting me stay a few more days while I get all the paperwork in order. With this ridiculous Bigfoot Festival in town, there are no open rooms between here and Charleston."

Q'Bita wanted to scream. He'd just played her like a fiddle, knowing full-well that Allegro was the way to her heart. "Okay, you can stay, but I want you gone as soon as the ink dries on that paperwork."

The look of smug self-satisfaction on his face made her want to puke but he had just done her an immense favor, and for that she was willing to call a temporary truce.

"Is there anything else?" Q'Bita asked impatiently.

"Well, since you've asked, I was hoping that we could continue our discussion about our future."

"No."

"Well, that was kind of a rush judgement, don't you think?"

"No, I don't. I'm not sure what you thought was going to happen when you showed up here but let me be clear. As far as I'm concerned, the man I married died five years ago. You are a stranger to me. I don't understand how you could have done what you did and I'm not entirely sure I want to."

"I don't understand how you can say that, Q'Bita. I've already explained that I did what I did to protect you. You've lived a rather sheltered and privileged life. You have no concept of just how dangerous the real world is."

Q'Bita snorted out loud. "I guess you don't know me as well as you think you do. I'll have you know that in that last six months I've solved two murders, rescued Andy from kidnappers, and helped take down Gianni Marini and his smuggling gang."

Alain gave her an imperious and slightly annoyed look. "Oh, I'm aware alright. You also almost got yourself killed solving the first case, and your second case may have benefited your baboon of a fiancé but it didn't turn out quite so well for Henri, did it?"

Q'Bita had to hand to Alain, he sure knew how to open a wound.

"We're done here, and I'd appreciate it if you left your attorney's name with the front desk when you check out."

"Attorney? Q'Bita, let's not rush this. I know that my popping up here has been a shock but you need to take some time to process all this before making any decisions. We had a good life, and you don't belong here, in this place."

Q'Bita bristled at the way he'd practically spat the words 'this place'. She was tired and didn't want to continue this conversation.

"Alain, I refuse to discuss this any further. Thank you for what you did regarding Allegro."

She picked up the pie and left the kitchen without waiting for a reply.

***

She'd calmed down significantly by the time Andy arrived back at the Red Herring Inn. They snuggled on the couch while Andy filled her in on what had happened to Cane. He agreed with Cane's suspicion that someone had tampered with the ladder. He and Cane were going to install security cameras tomorrow, hoping it would deter any would-be vandals.

Allegro stirred from his favorite nap spot on Q'Bita's lap, made his way to Andy's chest, and settled in to continue his nap. Q'Bita suddenly remembered the good news but hesitated as she thought about the best way to tell Andy.

She could feel him watching her and it made her self-conscious.

"Something on your mind, babe?"

"Well, yes, but promise me you won't get upset."

Andy raised his right eyebrow at her and pulled a face. "If you have to ask then I'm guessing it involves Alain."

"That would be a good guess."

Andy sighed. "Will I want pie before or after I hear what he did now?"

"Probably both, but I have ice cream, if it helps."

She went to the kitchen and grabbed two bowls. She put an extra-large piece of caramel apple pie in the bottom of Andy's bowl. She topped it off with a double scoop of cinnamon ice cream and added some cherries to sweeten the deal. Cherries were another of Andy's favorites, and she wanted him in a good mood for as long as possible.

Allegro was awake and licking Andy's chin when she returned with the pie. "Dang it to hell, I'm going to miss this little guy. I tried to not get attached but he won me over. Maybe we should think about getting a puppy of our own."

"Well, since you brought it up… It seems that Alain did some negotiating and Gianni Marini has agreed to let us keep Allegro."

She kept a close eye on Andy's face, trying to gauge his reaction, but his face gave no clue as to what he was thinking. She reminded herself not to play poker with him anytime soon.

Andy remained quiet a few seconds longer, and when he spoke his tone was somber. "Before I ask, remember that I didn't get mad, just like you asked, so I'm hoping you won't either."

"Okay, that's fair."

"Not that I'm an expert when it comes to your ex, but based on what I've seen so far, I'm guessing he didn't do this out of the kindness of his heart, so what else is behind this?"

Q'Bita braced herself and decided to be completely truthful with Andy. If they were going to build a life together, she wanted it to be built on a better foundation than her first marriage was.

"He wanted me to allow him to stay here at the Red Herring Inn until the transfer process details have been completed."

"And?"

"And he wanted to discuss reconciliation."

Q'Bita could see the anger working itself up in Andy's posture.

"Before you get upset, I promise you I made it clear to him that if he stayed, I didn't want to see or hear from him again. I asked him to leave his attorney's contact information at the front desk when he checks out. The second that man's plane leaves the ground, I plan to have Kent Haskell start looking into how I can legally remove Alain from my life."

"Do you think he'll listen and just go back to France and stay there?"

"Honestly? I have no idea. He's obviously not the person I thought I married, and I have no idea how his mind works. On the bright side, you said it would only take a day or two, and I'm sure I can manage to avoid him until he's gone."

"Speaking of gone, is there any more pie or is it gone?"

Relief washed over her as she went to the kitchen to grab the last slice of pie. She was finally starting to believe that the drama of the last few days would soon pass and she would be able to get back to planning her life without interruption.

Chapter 13

The next two days flew by as Q'Bita, her nana, Evie, and Rene prepared hundreds of pepperoni rolls and dozens of pans of mac-n-cheese for the inn's stand at the Bigfoot Festival. Andy had sacrificed himself and offered to coordinate the booth staffing. Q'Bita felt bad for him. She'd been stuck with the volunteer scheduling last year, and it had been like herding cats.

So far, she'd managed to successfully avoid Alain despite his attempts to thwart that. When Q'Bita ignored the note he'd left her in the cooking school, he turned to Jamie and tried to get him to convince her that she was being unreasonable. His attempt at manipulating her bestie hadn't gotten him any further than his note.

"Hello, Earth to Q'Bita? Snap out of it, sister, and pay attention. The last three pepperoni rolls you passed me are just sad-ass empty dough pockets."

Q'Bita blinked and looked at Rene like he'd been speaking in tongues.

"For the love of llamas, I need a break. You people are working me like a pack mule, and I haven't had a nap in days. I'm going to retire to the veranda. One of you be a dear and fetch me some sweet tea. I'm parched."

As Rene sauntered away, he called back through the screen door, "Don't forget the twist of lemon and an extra glass of ice. Cookies would be nice, too."

"I'll get you your cookies, princess, but have fun guessing which ones I licked and which ones I didn't," Evie yelled after him.

Q'Bita sat down on the closest stool and listened as her nana and Evie continued to plot against Rene. Alain was so wrong; this was her happy place, and she couldn't imagine being anywhere but here.

***

Q'Bita and Andy had just finished dinner and had kicked back, relaxing on the couch with Allegro, when Q'Bita's phone dinged. She glanced at the screen and saw a 911 text from Jamie.

"Crap, now what?"

Andy gave her a curious look. "Sounds like trouble."

"It's Jamie. He says it urgent. I'm not sure I have the energy for urgent tonight."

"A business owner's work is never done."

"Good thing you're cute, Mr. Hansen."

Q'Bita dialed Jamie's cell and he picked up on the first ring.

"I just got off the phone with a lovely French woman named Monique. She was calling to extend Alain's reservation an additional five days."

"What?"

Q'Bita shouted loud enough that she woke Allegro and made Andy jump.

"Calm down. I told her that I'd have to check our books and would get back to her within the hour. I wasn't about to extend his reservation without talking to you first."

"Did Monique say why he wanted to extend his reservation?"

Q'Bita saw Andy's head snap in her direction. She tried to give him her best 'I'm sorry' look but she could tell it hadn't had the desired effect.

"She only said that his business here had not concluded as expected and he would need to extend his stay an additional five days."

"Okay, thanks for the heads-up. I need to talk to Andy, and I'll call you back in a few."

Q'Bita hung up and immediately started to bite her lower lip.

"I gather there's an issue with Alain?" Andy said with an edge to his tone.

"Yes, apparently his business is not concluded. Not sure what that means but he wants to stay five more days."

"If you want, I can call Mikey and see if he knows what's going on."

Q'Bita considered it for a minute. She didn't want Andy to abuse his relationship with Mike Collins but she didn't want to be manipulated by Alain either.

"If it isn't too much trouble. I would rather know the whole story before making a decision."

"Consider it done. I think this little guy could use a potty break. Why don't you take him out while I see what I can get out of Mikey?"

Q'Bita leaned in and gave Andy a kiss on the cheek. "I love you."

Andy chuckled. "I love you too. Almost as much as I love pie."

Q'Bita picked up Allegro and tucked him under one arm, and tossed a throw pillow at Andy on her way to the door.

She checked in with Jamie on her way outside and told him that she would make the call back to Monique. They chatted a few minutes and then she headed outside so Allegro could handle his business.

They'd only been outside for a few minutes when Alain arrived. She thought about grabbing Allegro and heading back inside before he got out of the car but he'd already seen her and was waving her down as he jumped out of the car.

"Q'Bita, can I have a word with you, please?"

"If this is about your reservation, Jamie is checking our availability but I can't promise that we can accommodate you."

"We both know that you can accommodate me if you wanted to. After all, I am your husband, and last I knew you had a suite here."

Q'Bita closed her eyes and inhaled deeply through her nose. When she opened her eyes, she threw daggers at Alain. "If you're insinuating that I should allow you to stay with me, I think you should seek medical assistance, because you've obviously had a stroke and there's not enough oxygen getting to your brain."

"You've developed a somewhat acerbic attitude since you've returned to the States. No doubt a by-product of the quality of people you've been spending your time with. I imagine it's exhausting. You should really consider coming back to Europe with me, where you can work on finding your old self again. I liked her better."

Q'Bita balled her right hand into a fist and showed it to Alain. "How's your nose feeling?"

Alain took a few quick steps backward. "There's no need to resort to violence."

"I don't know, I'd kind of like to see her sock you in the snoot again," Andy said as he descended the front steps and came toward them.

Q'Bita was secretly delighted to see the look of annoyance on Alain's face as Andy approached.

"I would greatly appreciate it if you did not encourage her poor manners."

"Are all French people condescending a-holes or is it just you?"

Alain had turned beet-red and looked like he might blow a fuse any second. As much as Q'Bita disliked him, she didn't want to risk Andy getting in any more trouble if this went any further downhill.

"Okay, boys, this has been fun but I think we should say good night and finish this conversation later. Andy and I have a full day tomorrow and we need to get up early."

"You a hunter, Alain? Maybe you should join the hunt. There have been a few recent sightings. This just might be the year we bag a Bigfoot."

Q'Bita tried not to laugh at the thought of how miserable Alain would be on a Bigfoot hunt. He was definitely more the wine- or art-festival type.

"It was kind of you to offer but I don't believe in cryptids and would rather not contract Lyme's disease chasing a myth."

"Suit yourself but you're gonna miss out on some good 'shine and Q'Bita's pepperoni rolls."

"Sounds utterly charming," Alain said sarcastically.

Q'Bita decided to use the pause in conversation to pick up Allegro and steer Andy towards the front porch.

"Wait, Q'Bita. You haven't told me if you're extending my reservation yet."

Q'Bita looked back over her shoulder and then shrugged. "I haven't decided yet."

Andy laughed out loud. "Have I told you lately that I love you?"

***

The next morning came way too soon. Q'Bita shut off the alarm and caught the scent of fresh coffee. She rolled over and noticed the other side of the bed was empty so she got up and made her way to the kitchen. Andy was leaning against the counter, looking at his phone.

"Good morning, sunshine. Can I get you some coffee?"

"Why on earth are you up already, and why are you so chipper?"

Andy flashed her a huge smile. "It's hunt day. I look forward to this every year. It's a Castle Creek tradition, and seeing as how I'm not the Sheriff, I can actually enjoy myself, for once."

A wave of sadness washed over Q'Bita as Andy's words sank in. It had been a rough couple of weeks since Jock's murder. She knew that Andy missed his grandfather more than he was letting on, and the resulting fallout had been more than most people could handle. Andy had been suspended from the job he loved, his biggest rival was now the acting Sherriff, and the key witness in the case was about to leave the country instead of testifying thanks to Q'Bita's not-so-dead husband.

Good Lord, just thinking about it made her want to crawl back into bed and hide.

"What's on your mind, gorgeous?" Andy asked.

"Sorry, just thinking about everything you've been through the last few weeks and how proud I am of how strong you are. I don't tell you often enough how much I respect and admire you."

Andy chuckled and gave her a semi-embarrassed smile. "That's very kind of you to say. Any chance you wanna run my election campaign? I could use the PR."

"Ugh, with everything going on I'd almost forgotten about that. I guess you'll need to start planning soon. I'm more than willing to help in any capacity."

"I'm glad you said that, because I've thinking of running on a pie platform. With my good looks and your amazing pie, Chance won't stand a chance."

Q'Bita groaned then rolled her eyes as Andy laughed at his own bad humor. "Any chance I can get that coffee now?"

"Ha, you're cute. I see what you did there but maybe you should stick to pie and let me do the comedy," Andy said as he handed her a mug and a spoon.

Q'Bita pinched him and he yelped. "Ouch. You're mean when you first wake up, woman. I'm going to take Allegro out before you start in on him."

"Don't you have to be tough to be Sheriff?"

Andy shot her a pathetic look that she assumed was supposed to be his offended look. It needed work, to say the least. She waived bye as Andy and Allegro headed out the door.

She took a few sips of coffee, grabbed her cell phone, and headed to the couch to call Jamie. Mike Collins had gotten back to Andy last evening and explained that there was a delay with Gianni Marini's paperwork because his attorneys were now involved and mucking up the process. As much as she hated the idea of Alain staying any longer, she and Andy both agreed that it would be easier to know what he was up to if he were staying at the Red Herring Inn.

"Hiya, Q'B-Doll. What's shaking?"

"I just wanted to give you a quick call before the festival and let you know that I called Monique back last night and let her know that we'll be extending Alain's reservation."

"How does the hunky lawman feel about this?"

"He's about as thrilled as I am but we both agree that Alain can't be trusted and it's best to keep your enemies as close as possible, I guess."

"I second that, and it gives me easier access to him if I need to go all stealth mode on his ass."

Q'Bita laughed but made a mental note of Jamie's enthusiasm for the task. Jamie's hacking skills had come in handy more than once these last few months, and she wouldn't hesitate to involve him if it became necessary.

A knock at the door interrupted their conversation. Q'Bita crossed the room and pulled open the door, expecting it was Andy and Allegro, but was surprised to see Rene.

"Why aren't you dressed yet? Wait, unless that's what you're planning on wearing, in which case my first question should have been, you're not seriously planning on wearing that, are you? Your sense of style is definitely more hobo than Boho. I honestly have no idea how you snagged a dreamboat like Andy Hansen with your wardrobe disabilities. Europe was wasted on you, Q'Bita."

Q'Bita was still standing next to the open door, holding the phone, as Rene walked into the kitchen and helped himself to coffee. She turned back to the unfinished conversation with Jamie. "So, in case you missed any of that, Rene's here. I should probably go so I can give him my undivided attention while he finishes his pep talk."

"Better you than me, sister."

"Oh, don't worry. The booth isn't very big so you'll get to spend plenty of quality time with Queen Diva this weekend."

Q'Bita hung up and was about to close the door when Andy returned. Allegro started to bark as soon as he saw Rene.

"How much longer is that mangy canine terrorist going to be

freeloading here?"

Andy handed Allegro to Q'Bita. "You got this? I'm gonna go find Beecher and see if he needs any help with the hunt stuff."

"He's in the barn, fussing over those wretched chickens. I swear no one around this place respects Rolfie's rightful spot at the top of the food chain."

Andy kissed Q'Bita's cheek and whispered, "Good luck. Call me if you need back-up."

Q'Bita waited for Andy to leave and then made her way to the kitchen with Allegro. She fed him and then decided to deal with Rene. "So, I have some good news. Gianni has agreed to let me keep Allegro."

"How is that good news? In case you've forgotten, he and Rolfie are not exactly besties, and Rolfie was here first."

"Rolfie is a big kitty, Rene, and I'm sure they'll learn to love each other before you know it."

"If Rolfie ends up with ticks or rabies, you'll be hearing from my vet. Just saying. Now, will you please put on something presentable so we can get moving? I need to make sure that our booth projects the proper aesthetic before it's mobbed by hangry hillbillies."

Q'Bita closed her eyes and took a deep breath. She had a feeling it was going to be a very long weekend.

Chapter 14

Q'Bita was surprised at the turnout. The festival had drawn a much bigger crowd then they'd anticipated, and they were selling pepperoni rolls so fast she was beginning to worry they didn't have enough to last the day, let alone the weekend. Things finally slowed down a bit once the hunt started, and everyone in the booth decided to take a much-needed break.

Hadleigh was her usually peppy self and didn't seem the least bit tired. Q'Bita was fading fast and could see that her nana, Evie, and Rene were all looking like they could use a nap.

"Okay, I don't know about the rest of you, ladies, but I've personally gone from dewy to moist, and it is not a zone that I'm comfortable in. I have things sticking to parts of me that may never peel back off. I swear to you, I feel a severe case of prickly heat rash developing somewhere that one doesn't want to scratch or apply ointment in public. If my sparkling personality wasn't the driving force behind the success of this operation, I'd be home, soaking in a tepid oatmeal bath as we speak."

Evie grunted. "So, Your Majesty, was it your sparkling personality that kicked in when you told Trish Holden that her four children were four too many and that children were best when neither seen nor heard? 'Cause I don't think she found you all that shiny."

It was her nana's turn next. "I don't know what you're caterwauling about, Evie. You're just as bad as he is."

Evie did her best to look offended while laughing. "I have no idea what you're on about, Liddy Lou."

"Well, let me refresh your aged memory, then. I'm fairly certain that Judge Tanner didn't appreciate you insinuating that his wife had some gypsy in her and accusing her of trying to confuse you into giving her more change then she was owed."

"Maybe so, but I see it didn't stop him from coming back a second time and ordering three more pepperoni rolls, now, did it?"

This back-and-forth continued a few more minutes, then the crowd started up again.

Sales stayed steady, but not overwhelming, for the rest of the afternoon. They had just sat down for another break around dusk when the sound of sirens drew their attention.

Q'Bita saw Chance and Mike Collins both fly by with full lights and sirens going, followed by an ambulance. Whatever was happening, it seemed urgent. Her breath caught in her chest when she saw them taking a hard turn onto the access road leading to the main field where the hunt had been staged.

"Dear Lord, I hope something hasn't happened on the hunt. I always worry when too many of those boys get to drinking and traipsing around those woods that sooner or later one of them is going to get hurt," Liddy Lou said.

Q'Bita felt a little nauseous as the crowd started to make their way towards the staging area. She jumped when her cell phone buzzed in her pocket. She glanced quickly at the screen and saw a text from Andy. *"We have a situation. I need you to keep Evie over there. Do not let her come over here. I'll call you as soon as I can."*

She quickly shoved her phone back into her pocket and avoided eye contact with the others.

"Everything okay, darling?" her nana asked.

She hated lying to her nana but she didn't want to let on that anything was wrong.

"Yep. It was just a wrong number."

Her nana gave her a look that said 'I know you're lying but I won't push it'. They all watched as the crowd continued to gather near the staging area. About ten minutes later, the Bishop Search and Rescue team arrived.

"Okay, I'm no expert, but that's not a good sign. Someone must be lost or hurt really badly," Hadleigh said.

Evie started to say something but the sound of a large, low-flying helicopter drowned her out. Q'Bita looked up and saw the HealthNet 5 helicopter. It passed directly over the booth and landed on the far side of the staging area.

"I'd say someone's hurt for sure," Evie muttered.

"Sweet Jesus on a buttermilk biscuit, you don't think it's one of our men, do you? I may be the picture of perfection in mourning wear but I am too young to be a widow."

"Let's not jump to conclusions, Rene. The men in our lives are all experienced hunters and know how to do things safely. More than likely, it's just a broken leg or heat stroke. Nothing too traumatic."

"I hope you're right, Liddy Lou. I ain't as young as Princess Pound Cake here but if I'm going to have to put Putnam in the ground, I want it to be my doing."

"Evelyn Louise Newsome, you don't mean that and you know it."

"Oh, relax, Liddy Lou. We both know Put's too damn ornery to die. He plans on sticking around and pissing me off until my last breath."

Q'Bita pulled her phone back out and was getting ready to text Andy when Hadleigh said, "Look, here come Beecher and Jamie."

"Oh, thank you, Jesus," Rene said with an over-exaggerated exhale.

Q'Bita noticed Liddy Lou and Evie exchange nervous glances.

"Just Beecher and Jamie? Where's the rest of them?" Evie asked.

As Beecher and Jamie came closer, Q'Bita could see a dark red stain on Beecher's vest. Hadleigh moved closer and whispered, "Is that blood?"

"I think so," Q'Bita whispered back.

"I have a really bad feeling about this."

"Me too, Hadleigh."

Rene bolted out of the booth and rushed towards Beecher. He stopped quickly and let out a girly yelp. "OMG, please tell me that's not your blood. Are you wounded? Is it fatal? Dear Lord, I feel faint."

Beecher closed his eyes and pinched the bridge of his nose. He shot Rene an exasperated look and held up his free hand. "Rene, I'm fine but I need you to pull it together for the next few minutes."

For once in his over-the-top life, Rene stood still and remained quiet. Beecher patted his husband on the shoulder as he walked by and bent in to kiss him gently on the cheek. "Thank you. I promise I will let you fuss over me all you want when we get home."

Q'Bita could feel the tension building within the booth as everyone waited for Beecher to explain what had happened.

Beecher and Jamie made their way into the booth and Hadleigh handed them each a bottle of cold water. Beecher downed his in a single gulp. He wiped his mouth on the back of his hand and then cleared his throat. He took a few steps toward Evie, and Q'Bita saw her begin to shake.

"Evie, maybe you should sit down," Beecher said softly.

"I'm okay, Beecher. Just tell me what happened to my Put."

"Put's fine, Evie," Beecher said.

"Wait. If the old goat is fine, then why should I sit down?"

Beecher and Jamie exchanged a look that Q'Bita couldn't quite read.

"Because, Evie, it's Cane."

Evie let out a wail and collapsed into Liddy Lou's arms.

"No, no, no, not my Cane. Please, not my Cane."

Q'Bita choked back a sob and noticed that Hadleigh was also in tears. Jamie walked over and put an arm around each of them and held them tight.

"How bad is it?" Q'Bita asked quietly.

"It's bad, Q'B-Doll. I'm not sure if he's going to make it."

Her nana walked Evie over to a stool and sat her down but didn't let go. Beecher grabbed some napkins and passed them to Evie. She blew her nose life a foghorn then took a deep breath. "Okay, I'm good now. Tell me what's happened to Cane."

"He and Put were down in a creek bed looking for tracks. Someone with a bow took a shot at something, and the arrow hit Cane."

"What so you mean, hit him?" Evie asked.

Beecher bent down on one knee in front of Evie and reached for her hand. "I'm sorry, Miss Evie, the last thing I want to do is upset you."

"I know that, Beecher, but I want to know."

"The arrow hit Cane in the back, just below the left shoulder blade. It went pretty deep, and he's lost a lot of blood."

"Where's Putnam?" Evie asked calmly.

"Orvis thinks Put may have a mild case of shock so the EMS crew are checking him out now. Andy stayed with him and is going to drive you both to the hospital as soon as EMS clears Put."

"I want to see him. He's gonna need me."

Beecher glanced at their nana and she nodded. "I'll gather your things, Evie."

Q'Bita helped her nana find Evie's purse and cell phone. "Nana, why don't you go with Beecher and Evie? The rest of us will close up the booth and meet you back home."

A few minutes later her phone rang. She pulled it from her pocket and was relieved to see it was Andy.

"Hi, sweetheart. How's Put?"

"Physically, he's okay, but he's taking this pretty hard. I've never seen him show any emotion but he's a wreck, Q'Bita. He loves Cane like a son, and I hate to think what will happen if Cane doesn't pull through."

"Gosh, this is awful, Andy. Do they know who it was that shot the arrow?"

"No, not yet. We had all separated into smaller groups, and by the time anyone heard Put calling for help there was no one around. Chance and Mike are taking statements and working the scene so hopefully we'll know something soon."

"I just can't believe that someone would be so careless with something as dangerous as a bow. How could they have mistaken Cane for a paper target?"

"That's just it, Q'Bita, Put and Cane weren't anywhere near one of the paper targets. No one should have been shooting in that area. We put all the paper targets up on the main trail, and they were all out in the open. The rules stated that all participants were to stay on the main trail and could only fire on the targets in the presence of a Hunt Guide."

"Why did Put and Cane leave the main trail, then?"

"When our group stopped for lunch, Jake Morgan was carrying on again about that damn Bigfoot footage and how it was going to be worth a fortune to some big TV network show. Cane was teasing him about it. Jake got all worked up and said he could prove it was real and that he could take us to the Bigfoot nest. Damn fool got us lost looking for the trail, so Beecher suggested we all break off into smaller groups and try to figure out where we were."

"Wait, so if you guys all broke off from the main group, does that mean that—"

Andy finished her sentence. "Yes, it means that whoever shot that arrow was probably someone in our group. That's what makes this whole thing even worse than it already is."

"Oh my God, I think I'm going to be sick. How could this happen?"

"I don't know, babe, but I have to go. Beecher and Liddy Lou just got here with Evie, and I need to get her and Put to the hospital. I'll call you as soon as I know anything."

They said their goodbyes and Q'Bita hung up. She sat down and let their conversation sink in. They had all been through so much in the last few months, and while she'd firmly believed that God never gave you more than you could handle in a day, she was starting to wonder if God knew they weren't superheroes.

***

Andy called a few hours later to let her know that her nana was going to stay at the hospital with Put and Evie and that he was headed back to the scene.

"Do you think Chance is going to let you help with the investigation?"

"No, of course not, but I'm hoping he'll let Mikey take my statement and maybe I can get him to spill the beans as to what they've found so far."

"What's going to happen to whoever did this?"

"I'm not sure, Q'Bita. Hopefully, Cane pulls through and it turns out this was all just an accident but we'll have to wait and see, I guess."

"You say that like there's a possibility that this could have been something other than an accident. You don't really think someone did this on purpose, do you?"

"I sure hope not, babe, but it seems mighty suspicious that someone messes with the ladder in Put's barn and then a few days later this happens. It's a long shot, but the cop in me says there might be something more going on here."

"But who would want to hurt Cane? He doesn't seem like a guy with many enemies."

"That's the part I'm struggling with. Cane and Put were wearing the same gear today. From a distance it would have been hard to tell which one was which, especially if their backs were to the shooter. When you factor in that the ladder was in Put's barn, that leads me to question if the target was really Cane or it could have been Put."

Q'Bita felt a rising panic. Put Newsome wasn't exactly cuddly and well-liked. She had no problem imagining that the list of people with a grudge against him was as long as her arm, but what worried her most was the fact that the only person who'd recently threatened to kill Put was her own brother.

"You still there, babe?" Andy asked.

"Ya, sorry. Andy, please tell me you were with Beecher when this happened."

The fact that Andy didn't immediately answer filled her with dread.

"Q'Bita, don't start panicking. I'm sure Beecher had nothing to do with this."

"You weren't with him, then?"

"No. When Beecher suggested that we all split up, Put and Cane took the creek bed and Jake Morgan, Orvis, and I took the upper ridge line. Beecher took the middle ground."

"So Beecher was alone?"

"Ya, but like I said, I'm sure he had nothing to do with this, babe."

"Of course not. I was just hoping there was someone who could vouch for him."

After they hung up, Q'Bita tried to calm her nerves with a cup of tea but she couldn't shake the feeling that things were about to go from bad to worse when her phone rang again.

"Hey, Jamie. What's up?"

"Hey, Q'B-Doll. I'm down at the front desk and I need your help with something."

"Sure. What can I do?"

"Well, if you can pull an extra room out of thin air, that would be a good start."

"Sorry. I'm good but I'm not that good."

"I was afraid you'd say that. Henri's wife just walked in, and she was hoping to get a room. I had no idea he was even married. Did you?"

"No, I had no idea. Give me a second and I'll be right down."

Q'Bita ran a comb through her hair and slapped on some lip gloss. She hurried down the stairs and found a stunning woman standing next to Jamie. She looked up as Q'Bita walked toward them.

"Q'Bita, this is Mariah Sinclair, Henri's wife."

"Bon jour, Q'Bita. Thank you for coming so quickly."

Not only was she stunning, her voice was like honey, and Q'Bita loved the way she pronounced her name, Coo-Bee-Duh.

"It's a pleasure to meet you. I'm so sorry for everything you've been through. I'm sure you must be exhausted."

"I've just come from seeing Henri, and fortunately he's doing better. The doctors are hopeful, which is a relief. I'm so sorry to impose upon you but I don't know anyone here in the States and wasn't sure where else to go."

"It's no problem at all. I'm sure we can find a way to make this work."

Q'Bita paused for a minute as a wicked idea came to her.

"Jamie, I have an idea. Do you know if Alain is in his room?"

"No. He went into Charleston but he should be back soon."

"Good. Send someone up to clear his room and prepare it for Mariah."

Q'Bita could see Jamie almost swallow his tongue and she had to stifle a giggle.

"Oh no, I wouldn't want you to inconvenience anyone else on my behalf," Mariah said.

"Oh, trust me, it's no inconvenience at all. The current occupant has more than overstayed his welcome," Q'Bita replied. "Why don't you come with me and I'll get you some tea and a bite to eat until your room's ready."

As they walked away, Jamie asked what he should do with Alain's things. Q'Bita excused herself and walked back to where Jamie was standing.

"Have them taken to the barn. There's an old bunk in the loft that Rolfie uses for his afternoon nap. I'm sure it will do Alain just fine."

"I'm not sure what's gotten into you, Q'B-Doll, but I like it. Please tell me that I can be the one to inform your ex of his upgrade."

"Done. What are besties for? Oh, and don't forget to leave a chocolate on his pillow. We want all our guests to know just how much we care."

Q'Bita walked back to Mariah Sinclair and led her to the kitchen.

"How do you like your tea?" Q'Bita asked.

"I usually drink rooibos, but Henri tells me he's become fond of your American sweet tea."

"I just made a batch of sweet tea with mint this morning. Would you like to try some?"

"Please, don't go to any trouble for me. I feel like I'm imposing on you already."

"Nonsense. I can't imagine what you've been going through, so please don't hesitate to ask for anything you need."

Q'Bita could see tears welling up in Mariah's eyes and she felt herself getting choked up, too. She sat the glasses and the pitcher of sweet tea on the counter and placed a hand on Mariah's shoulder.

"I'm not sure if you know this or not but your husband saved my life."

Mariah looked up and Q'Bita could see a mixture of surprise and confusion on her face.

"I'm glad to hear that but I still don't understand what he was doing here in the first place. I asked the woman who called me from Interpol but she said she had no details and only knew that Henri had been shot. He's an administrative assistant, not a field agent. It just doesn't make sense."

"I wish I could tell you more. I'm not sure of much myself, but I do know someone who should be able to give you answers."

As if the mere thought of him had summoned him, Alain walked into the kitchen.

"Mention the devil and he shall appear," Q'Bita muttered.

"Oh, my apologies. I didn't realize you had company."

Q'Bita watched as Mariah and Alain exchanged glances. As far as she could tell, they did not recognize each other.

"I take it you two haven't met before now."

She waited for one or the other to correct her but neither did.

"Mariah, this is Alain La Roche, but you may know him as Victor Cortez."

She could see that Alain's alias was familiar to Mariah.

"Alain, this is Mariah Sinclair, Henri's wife."

"You're Henri's boss?"

Alain moved closer to Mariah and reached out to shake her hand.

"Yes. It's a pleasure to finally meet you. Your husband speaks highly of you."

Mariah returned his compliment with a slap across the face.

"Then you're the one responsible for what's happened to my Henri."

Though they'd only just met, Q'Bita decided she liked this woman already.

Alain recoiled in shock. "What is it with you women and your violent reactions?"

A look of embarrassment came over Mariah as she turned to Q'Bita.

"I'm sorry. You must think I'm awful."

"Actually, no. I gave him that broken nose a few days ago. He has that effect on people."

"You're not funny, Q'Bita," Alain snarked.

"I wasn't trying to be. I think you should consider yourself lucky that all she did was slap you."

"She's right. I want to choke you, but first I'd like to know why you sent my husband here in the first place and how he ended up in that warehouse."

Alain tried his best to explain but Q'Bita was fairly certain his story wasn't sitting well with Henri's wife.

"So let me get this straight. You are a selfish and foolish man who got yourself exposed, then faked your own death to hide from a dangerous man. Now you're tired of hiding so you manipulated my husband into doing your dirty work, knowing full-well who he was dealing with and not really caring that he was neither fully trained nor ready to be in the field. Is that correct?"

Q'Bita watched in delight as Alain squirmed under Mariah's gaze.

"Q'Bita, a little help?"

"I don't think there's anything I can say that will help you out of this one, Alain."

Alain's upper lip curled like he was smelling bad cheese, and Q'Bita desperately hoped that Mariah would slap him again just for fun.

"Very well, then. Perhaps we should finish this discussion later, when you've both had time to calm down."

Alain turned to walk away but Mariah stood and blocked his path.

"Mr. La Roche, you can try to avoid the truth if you choose, but know that if my husband doesn't make a full recovery, this man you're running from will be the least of your worries."

Q'Bita swore she saw a quiver pass through Alain, and once again realized just how much she liked this woman. She had moxy for days.

"Um, Alain, not to prolong your visit but I'm assuming that you came in here to see me for something."

"Yes, of course. What is this nonsense about my room being moved?"

"Oh, that. Mariah will be taking your room. You're being moved to the loft."

"What loft? I've made several security sweeps of this building and I haven't seen anything that could be described as a loft."

"That's because it's in the barn."

"Are you insane? I'm not some local inbred farmer, and will not be sleeping in a barn."

"Suit yourself. I said you could stay. I never said where."

"Q'Bita, I understand that you're not happy with me right now but this is beyond unreasonable."

"I don't know, sounds reasonable to me," Mariah said.

Alain stormed out of the kitchen without saying anything else. Q'Bita poured them another glass of iced tea and made Mariah a sandwich. They had just finished eating when Jamie popped in to say that Alain's things had been moved and the room was ready for Mariah.

***

After Q'Bita got Mariah settled in, she decided to take Allegro for a quick walk before bedtime. They'd just made it to the porch when she saw Chance Holleran's SUV entering the drive. He pulled up and made a show of parking on the grass, then he stepped out of the SUV and sneered at her.

"Evening, Q'Bita. Know where I can find Beecher?"

"I don't keep tabs on my brother. Have you tried knocking on his door or maybe calling him to see if he's here before just showing up?"

"How the hell Hansen puts up with your insolent attitude, I will never know, but you best watch yourself with me, Q'Bita. As much trouble as you and your family find themselves in, it would best to not make an enemy of me."

Q'Bita was about to pull an Andy and tell Chance to go get bent when Beecher and Rene pulled in the driveway. Beecher stopped his truck and got out.

"Everything okay, Q'Bita?"

"No, everything is not okay, Beecher. I was just explaining to your sister how you people need to start showing me a little respect. Things are changing, and I plan to be keeping this badge right where it is. Now, if you don't mind, you and I have some things to discuss."

"Chance, it's late. Can this wait until tomorrow?" Beecher asked.

"Afraid not. It's official Sheriff business. We can do it here or I can slap some cuffs on you and take you down to the station. It's up to you."

Q'Bita thought back to her conversation with Andy and the fact that Beecher had no one to vouch for him. Her heart started thumping faster, and the look of concern on Beecher's face was not helping.

"Okay, fine. Let me take Rene over to the cottage and I'll be right back."

"Good choice. I was afraid if I had to slap the cuffs on you, your wife might get all excited."

Beecher started to say something but stopped as Rene flung open the passenger door.

"Never mind, Beecher, I got this. First of all, there is nothing about you or your handcuffs that excite me. Second, I'm all man, sugar, and I don't need to keep Beecher prisoner to win his affection. Lastly, you can just park your keister right back in your SUV as my husband will not be answering any questions until Kent Haskell gets here."

"I'm sure Kent Haskell has better things to do than drive out here on a Saturday night, Rene."

"Actually, I called him as soon as I saw you standing here. Every time you show up here it's bad news, and it usually requires a lawyer."

***

Twenty minutes later Q'Bita was sitting in the kitchen, watching Rene come unglued. "What's taking so long, Q'Bita? You don't think Chance is working Beecher over, do you? Beecher may look all manly farm hand on the outside but he bruises easily."

"Rene, relax. I'm sure Chance is just asking Beecher for the details of what happened with Cane. Besides, Chance is probably not foolish enough to do anything inappropriate with Kent Haskell sitting right there."

"Probably? Dear God, you don't think they'll use thumb screws, do you? Do they even still do that or is it just bamboo shives now?"

Q'Bita had to force herself not to face-plant into the counter in frustration.

"Rene, this is Castle Creek, not a POW camp. I'm sure Beecher is just fine."

Q'Bita heard the sound of tires crunching gravel just outside the door.

A few seconds later Andy walked in, and she could tell from the look on his face that he was already angry.

"Sorry, I got here as fast as I could. Where are they?"

Q'Bita stood up and placed one hand on Andy's chest. She could feel his heart racing through the fabric.

"Relax. Everything is just fine. Kent Haskell is here, too, so Chance will have to play this by the book."

Q'Bita felt some of the tension release in Andy's chest.

"Um, excuse me. Can we focus on the distraught spouse now, or is this going to be all about you two?"

"Hello, Rene."

"Don't hello me, Andrew. Why did you barrel in here all fired up? What aren't you saying?"

Once Rene stopped rapid-firing questions at Andy, Q'Bita convinced them both to sit down so they could all discuss things calmly.

"I went back out to the scene and talked to Mikey. Based on what they've been able to piece together so far, this isn't looking like an accident."

Rene sucked in a breath so hard he almost toppled backwards off his stool.

"You mean someone did this to Cane on purpose? Certainly no one thinks Beecher would do anything to hurt Cane. I mean, they're practically besties."

"Of course not, Rene. Everyone knows Beecher wouldn't hurt Cane."

Andy had suddenly gotten very quiet and was staring down at his hands, seemingly fascinated with his own fingers.

"They do know that, right, Andy?" Q'Bita asked.

"Yes. No one thinks that Beecher was trying to hurt Cane."

Q'Bita sensed a 'but' coming and she wasn't sure she was going to like it.

"There are some folks, though, who aren't so convinced that Cane was the intended target," Andy said quietly.

"Well, if the target wasn't Cane, then who was it?" Rene asked.

Q'Bita closed her eyes and took a deep breath to prepare herself for Rene's reaction.

"It's possible the intended target was Put."

Q'Bita watched as Andy's words sank in for Rene. She was surprised when Rene asked calmly, "How many people know about what happened between Beecher and Put the other day?"

"You mean how many people know that Beecher went after Put with a loaded shotgun and then threatened to kill him? Unfortunately, that would be just about everyone in town, and it's exactly why Chance is here now."

Every ounce of color drained from Rene's face and he began sobbing. Q'Bita tried comforting him but it was no use. When Beecher and Kent Haskell finally appeared in the kitchen, Rene had been through two boxes of tissues and Andy through most of a peach pie.

Rene threw himself off the stool toward Beecher so fast he almost took them both down. "Are you okay? Did Chance use excessive force? Do you still have thumbnails?"

"Rene, take it down a notch. I'm fine. It was just questions."

"Oh please, when it comes to Chance Holleran, it's never just questions. There's always an ulterior motive. Everyone knows that he's Red Dixon's lap dog, and Red would just love any excuse to nudge you out of your half of the Macie Dixon Line."

"Rene, you're being overly dramatic. Red may be a pain in the ass but he's kept his promise to stay out of mine and Hadleigh's business. I seriously doubt he has some big nefarious plan to oust me now."

"Beecher's right. I don't think Red had anything to do with this, for once. From what Mikey told me, it was Jake Morgan who brought up the run-in with Put."

"Jake Morgan? Why would Jake do that?" Q'Bita asked.

"I'm guessing it was to remove suspicion from himself," Andy said.

"Exactly. It was Jake who suggested we break off from the group. I still can't understand how he managed to get us lost in woods he's been hunting in for half a century. Seems odd in hindsight."

"If what Beecher's saying is true, couldn't that mean that Jack Morgan is somehow behind this?" Q'Bita asked.

"Sure, and if I were still Sheriff, I'd certainly be looking into that, but Mikey said that Chance heard Beecher's name and immediately decided he was the prime suspect."

"Suspect?" Rene screeched. "Does this mean you're going to have to go to trial? I didn't marry a felon, ergo I don't have a proper trial wardrobe. If it drags out too long, we're going to have to up the limit on our gold card."

Andy looked at Rene and then at Q'Bita. "Does he just lay awake at night thinking about ways to have a conniption fit?"

"Jest if you must, Andrew, but I will not have some hack, courtroom sketch artist rendering my portrait to look like trailer trash."

Kent Haskell cleared his throat. "Okay, let's not overreact. Right now, all Chance has is questions. If he had any evidence that Beecher had done anything wrong, he would have already arrested him. Given what I've gathered so far, there still isn't any definitive proof that Put, or Cane, were even targeted. This could all still turn out to be just an unfortunate accident.

"I hope you're right, Kent, but if not, I'm still confused as to why Jake Morgan would try to hurt anyone over something as silly as supposed Bigfoot footage."

Andy let out a low whistle.

"You sure don't know much about Bigfoot, Rene. If you did, you'd know that there are tons of folks out there who would pay a pretty penny for actual squatch footage."

"Your use of the term 'actual' speaks volumes regarding the depth of your gene pool. I suppose this folk ton you're referring to are the same intellectually challenged lot that purchase raccoon wieners online?" Rene quipped.

Q'Bita noticed Kent Haskell's face, and it was priceless. It was the same fuchsia color as her favorite rose.

"Actually, Rene, Andy's right. From what I hear, the footage that Jake has been bragging about is pretty high quality. He and Hank have a hot commodity on their hands and have been approached by several TV producers about selling it," Beecher said.

"Wait. Is this the same footage that Cane and Orvis were teasing Jake about during the Hunt Committee planning lunch?" Q'Bita asked.

"Yes, and to answer Rene's question, while we were on the hunt, Jake kept carrying on about how much money they were going to rake in, until Cane finally had enough and said he could prove the footage was a fake. Jake got angry and said he could show us proof. We all wanted to see what he was talking about so we followed him and, well, you know the rest," Beecher said.

"So, who has this footage now, and have any of you seen it?" Kent asked.

"I guess Hank Miller has it. I know Put saw it but I haven't," Andy said.

"Me neither," Beecher added.

"Okay, then my first order of business will be to follow up on this footage. If there's anything to it, I can probably argue that Chance hasn't considered all the other suspects. Might not get us anywhere but it's worth a shot," Kent said.

Q'Bita stayed in the kitchen with Rene while Andy and Beecher walked Kent to his car.

"So Kent has his plan but what's ours, Q'Bita? I know you well enough to know that the little hamster inside your head is already training for a 10K. There's no way you're going to just sit back and let Beecher take the fall for this."

"You know that I would never let anything happen to Beecher."

"Fine, then what time should I meet you and Jamie for our breakfast brainstorming session?"

Q'Bita laughed at how well her brother-in-law really did know her.

"As soon as I can get Andy out the door."

Before she and Andy went to bed, Q'Bita sent Jamie a text asking him to start digging into the supposed Bigfoot footage and to be at the cooking school at 8 a.m.

Chapter 15

Andy was up and out the door at first light, hoping to catch up with Clarity Fessler. As Castle Creek's only crime scene and lab tech, Clarity would be processing the evidence from Cane's case. Andy had been impressed with Clarity during her internship with his department, and had sweet-talked the Town Council into creating a permanent position for her. A fact Q'Bita hoped would allow Andy to get some inside scoop.

Jamie was ten minutes early, but Rene was running late, as usual. Q'Bita and Jamie were working on their second cup of coffee when Rene finally sauntered up the stairs at 8:45. He was wearing a pair of skintight red daisy dukes and a gauzy giraffe print shirt that looked like it belonged on a flamenco dancer. He'd capped off this ensemble with a pair of Christian Louboutin Lou Spikes Orlato high top sneakers that featured spike-encrusted toe boxes.

"Good morning, precious. What's with the studded shit-kickers?" Jamie asked with a chuckle.

"I'll have you know these are $700 shoes and just happen to scare the daylight out of those infernal feathered menaces that try to accost me every time I walk across this yard."

"For God's sake, Rene, they're just chickens. Their brain is the size of a pea. I'm pretty sure they're incapable of plotting your demise," Jamie said.

"Mock me if you must, but I'm telling you, those wretched creatures are one razor blade away from taking me out, and if there's one thing I've learned from living amongst country boys, it's that you never let your enemy strike first. That's why I bought these bad boys of fashion. I'm going to bring the cockfight to them before they bring it to me."

"Okay, you two, as amusing as this conversation has been, I think we're forgetting why we're here."

"Lord, yes, we have to keep my husband out of the hoosegow,

because I am not on board with the whole concept of monthly conjugal visits."

"Okay, TMI. Q'B-Doll's right, let's focus on our plan."

After an hour of planning they decided their first step was to track down the supposed Bigfoot footage. Jamie had a friend from his old hacker days who would be able to tell them if the footage had been faked.

In the meantime, Q'Bita and Rene were going to do some snooping to see if they could find out just how much Hank and Jack stood to gain if they sold the footage or how much they stood to lose if Cane exposed them.

Rene volunteered to work the grapevine at Fayleen's Day Spa and Paula's Posh Pet Grooming, which had not surprised Q'Bita or Jamie at all. Q'Bita was going to start with her evening cooking class. Hilde Sanders would be there, and everyone in Castle Creek knew that Hilde was the go-to gal for all things gossip.

When they'd finished running through the plan, Q'Bita sat back and sighed. "Well, the only thing missing from our plan is some way to get the inside scoop on what evidence has been discovered so far."

"What's the point of bedding the hunky lawman if he doesn't deliver the pillow talk?" Rene asked.

"I'm going to ignore the fact that you've just implied that I'm so devious that I would use sex as a ploy to get information out of my fiancé. Even if I was that kind of girl, I wouldn't get very far. If Andy suspects even for a second that we're doing our own investigation, he'll have a fit. You know he doesn't like me playing detective."

"I'm not saying I agree with Rene, but I would like to point out that, had we not stuck our noses in Jock's murder, not only would Carter have gotten away with it, Andy himself might not be here right now."

"I know that, Jamie, and I'm sure Andy does, too, but let's not forget that you and I could have been killed if it weren't for Henri. Andy knows how dangerous these types of investigations can be, and he gets worried when any of us get too involved," Q'Bita said.

"People, need I remind you that this isn't some random stranger we're trying to help? It's Beecher. Andy's just going to have to get over himself and deal with it. I refuse to sit on my pristinely waxed keister and hope that Chance Holleran has a sudden come-to-Jesus moment and decides to do what's right, for once."

"I promise you, Rene, all of us are going to help Beecher. We just have to be careful how we go about it."

Rene made a prune face and waved away her comment as if it had little substance. "Do what you want but I'm going to pitch a hissy all over this county until Beecher's name is cleared."

Q'Bita was relieved when Jamie quickly changed the subject. "So what time are your parents getting in?"

"Their plane lands in about an hour. Nana's picking them up, and they should be here by lunch."

"Did Liddy Lou have any update on Cane?" Jamie asked.

"Fortunately, he's stable and doing much better than the doctors expected."

"Wow, that's great news. I'm sure Evie and Put must be relieved."

"Yes, attempted murder is so much better than murder. I'm sure Beecher will only have to go to jail for a few decades vs. life," Rene snarked.

"Rene, I know you're worried but let's just focus on finding out what really happened. If we can figure this out, then Beecher will be off the suspect list and won't have to worry about anything."

Rene rolled his eyes at her, and she could tell that he had no intention of listening or being any less dramatic until Beecher was no longer a suspect.

"Okay, I think we all know what we need to do next, so let's get moving and we'll regroup tomorrow after I get Andy out the door."

After Rene left to go pre-primp for his spa day, Q'Bita and Jamie had another quick glass of lemonade.

"Q'Bita, do you really think Chance is going to be fair and look at the evidence objectively or do you think he's already made his mind up that it's Beecher and won't try any harder than he did with Jock's case?"

"I really don't know, Jamie. I want to believe that there's good even in someone like Chance Holleran but, honestly, I have a bad feeling that this is all going to get worse before it gets better."

***

Q'Bita passed time on the drive into town going back over everything she knew about the case so far, but nothing helpful came of it. She pulled into Rose's Bakery and got out of the car. A familiar voice from behind her caused her breakfast to do the cha-cha, and she hoped it would stay down.

"Hello, Spenser. What do you want?"

"My, my, Miss Block, no need to get testy. I was just wondering if you'd like to give me a quote regarding your brother's involvement in the Cane Jessop case."

What she wanted to give him was a swift kick in the peaches but Spenser Penn was not someone she wanted on her bad side until Beecher was in the clear.

"Put me down as no comment."

She tried to walk away but a camera man blocked her path and Spenser shoved a microphone in her face. She reached up and gently pushed it away.

"Spenser, will you please stop doing that? It's really annoying."

"It only bothers people who have something to hide," Spenser replied.

Q'Bita could feel herself getting angry but knew she couldn't explode. She'd been down this road with Spenser before, and it had never ended well for her. She faked right and the camera man took the bait. She zagged quickly to the left and shot through the opening. She could hear Spenser sputtering something but she ignored him as she pulled open the door and ducked into the bakery.

"Sugar, you just go on ahead and lock that door behind you. I don't serve his kind."

Rose Dawson was standing behind the counter, putting the final touches on a huge croque-en-bouche tower studded with bubblegum-pink and baby-blue macarons.

Q'Bita gasped as she took in the height and amazing detail work.

"Ain't she a beauty? It's for a baby shower gender reveal. Obviously, they're having twins."

"It's fabulous, Rose. I've seen hundreds of these but I don't think I've ever seen one so big or so beautiful."

"Thanks, darling. I'll definitely take that as a compliment, coming from you. I hear you're quite the talent yourself, especially when it comes to pies."

The compliment made Q'Bita chuckle. "I take it you've been talking to my fiancé."

"Fiancé? Well, I'll be. It's about time Andy Hansen found himself a good woman. Congratulations. I'm happy for you kids."

"Thanks, Rose. Once we set a date, I'll definitely be coming to see you about the cake, and now that I've seen this, I'm thinking a tower or two, as well."

Q'Bita noticed Rose glancing out the front window.

"Looks like Spenser gave up. I don't see him skulking around out there anywhere, so I'll grab your order and let you be on your way. I'm sure you probably want to get your errands done and get back to the Red Herring before every busybody in town starts pestering you about Cane Jessop. Such a tragedy, though. He's a nice boy. I hope he pulls through."

"Actually, he's doing much better than expected."

"Thank goodness. I know this sounds selfish but we need more business owners like Cane here in downtown. His willingness to network and try new marketing ideas has helped bring in a lot of fresh business. Some of these old buzzards like Hank Miller claim they don't want tourists here in town but I think they're wrong. I hear the old fool might have to sell the paint shop if he doesn't cash in on that fake sasquatch video. He'd rather run a scam on those TV people to get out of his financial problems than try something new to save a business that's been in his family for three generations. I just don't understand some folks."

Q'Bita didn't want to be nosey but she had to find out more.

"Wow, are things really that bad for Hank that he needs to sell?"

"Well, if Hilde Sanders is to be believed, Hank's had to cut hours just to cover payroll the last few weeks. She claims that Melvina over at the tax office told her that Hank's several quarters behind on his tax payments, as well. I tell you, Q'Bita, some of the old guard business owners here in town just can't come to terms with the fact that the way we do business has changed. If they don't adapt they're going to go under."

"No wonder he wants to sell that footage so badly. You're also not the first person who has said the footage is fake. Have you seen it?"

Rose threw back her head and howled. "Good Lord, no, but I've known Hank Miller and Jake Morgan since we were kids. Those two couldn't find each other's wieners with eight arms and two spotlights, let alone find the real Bigfoot. I'd bet my shop on that footage being as fake as your brother-in-law's tan."

Once Q'Bita stopped laughing, she made a mental note to get to know Rose and some of the in-town business owners better. If business was so scarce that one of them might be driven to commit murder, then maybe she could find a way to help once this whole mess was resolved.

While Rose went to grab her order, Q'Bita pulled out her phone and sent Jamie a quick text asking him to do some digging into Hank's finances. She felt guilty snooping into Hank's life but if it meant clearing Beecher, she was willing to live with the guilt.

"Here you go, sugar. Two dozen baguettes and a little something special for your nana. I know she likes my honey lavender madeleines so I saved her a few. I figure she and Evie might need a little comfort snack."

"Thank you, Rose. I'm sure it will be just what they need."

Q'Bita said her goodbyes and headed for her car. She kept an eye out for Spenser Penn but he seemed to have given up for now. She stowed the bakery order on the back seat and started toward the butcher shop when she heard Rene calling her name.

She looked up and saw him rushing toward her. He had Rolfie tucked under one arm and several shopping bags on the other. As they got closer, Q'Bita could see that Rolfie was wearing a spiked, giraffe-print collar and red tutu. She wasn't sure if Rene's insistence on dressing Rolfie like his twin was more amusing or concerning, but either way, she was fairly sure that Rolfie enjoyed it as much as Rene.

"Here, take him while I set these bags down. I'm about to faint from hunger and all this humidity."

"Rene, you just ate breakfast less than two hours ago. I personally saw you polish off two bagels and half a cantaloupe."

"Exactly. That's hardly enough to keep me going. Power-shopping burns more calories than you realize. I've also managed to learn some very interesting things this morning, and I'll gladly fill you in over lunch."

Q'Bita glanced at her watch and saw it was almost noon. She really shouldn't waste time but she was dying to hear what Rene had found out and to tell him what she'd learned about Hank.

"Okay. Where do you want to go?"

"I'll go anywhere except that hideous diner. I know you all love Dot Hendricks but she's a cat hater, and I've just had Rolfie's aura cleansed and chakras realigned. I don't want him exposed to all the negative energy."

Q'Bita looked down at the large feline in her arms and swore he rolled his eyes at her. Apparently, even Rolfie knew how ridiculous Rene could be at times.

"Since Beecher and Andy aren't here to veto me, let's do Ichi Hana. It's Rolfie's favorite. Most of these locals think fish is something you catch with corn, coat it in Ritz cracker crumbs, and fry into next week so I doubt we'll run into anyone we know."

Ten minutes later they were parked on the patio of Ichi Hana, looking over the menu. Several of the servers stopped by to say hello to Rolfie. Q'Bita had no idea he was such a celebrity around town.

After Rene ordered enough food for six people, she filled him in on what she'd learned from Rose.

"Interesting. My news is juicier. Seems Cane has himself a bit of baby-daddy drama going with Crystal Perdix."

"Wait, I thought Crystal was dating Mike Collins."

"Girl you need to keep up. Mike dumped Crystal months ago because he caught her banging Chance. Chance had no intention of keeping her so she moved on to Cane Jessop. Rumor has it that she pulled a Billie Jean on Cane."

"Okay, you lost me. What's a Billie Jean?"

"OMG, I really need to educate you on the finer points of gossip. Billie Jean, as in Michael Jackson. Billie Jean is not my lover… she's just a girl that thinks I am the one, but the kid is not my son."

Rene had belted out the lyrics so loud that everyone in the restaurant was now looking at them and Q'Bita wanted to crawl under the table and hide.

"Okay, you could have just said that she was trying to trap him and I would have understood."

"Yes, but my way had so much more pizzazz. You forget, I came from Broadway. I'm all about the dazzle, darling."

"Can we just get back to what this has to do with what happened to Cane?"

"Okay but do me a favor and at least try to keep up."

By the time Rene had finished his story their food had arrived. Q'Bita was grateful for the break. Listening to Rene tell a story could be exhausting, and something one should never do on an empty stomach or with a full bladder.

***

Andy and Mike Collins were deep in conversation about the details of the investigation so far when Chance stepped into the bullpen from his office.

"Hansen, you do realize that you no longer work here, right? I can't for the life of me figure out why your ugly face keeps showing up in my bullpen."

"Hey, Chance, where'd you come from?" Mike asked nervously.

"I came in through the parking lot. In case either of you've forgotten, I'm in charge around here now, and that comes with a parking space and my own entrance."

Andy was about to say something when the lobby door swung open and smacked the wall with a bang that reverberated all the way down the hall. Chance reached for his side arm and spun around just in time to see Crystal Perdix stomping toward the bullpen, looking mad as hell.

Crystal was a looker, but also a bit of a tramp. She was more pretty than bright, and existed in a constant swirl of drama that no sane man wanted a part of for more than a one-weekend stand.

She stopped halfway into the bullpen and planted her hands on her hips. She glared at the three of them then laid into Chance.

"Chance Holleran, why the hell are you just standing there looking at me like a lost kitten, and why isn't Maggie out there answering the phone? I've left several messages and no one is getting back to me."

Chance leaned against the edge of the desk and rubbed the bridge of his nose between his left thumb and index finger while he waited for Crystal to come up for air.

"Maggie left when Andy got shit-canned, so we don't have a receptionist any longer. Now, if you're done squawking like an angry chicken, I'll have Mikey take your complaint."

Mike Collins groaned, and this only made Crystal angrier.

"Don't either of you get uppity with me. The father of my unborn child was almost taken from this world yesterday, and you two are sitting here with your thumbs up your asses when you should be out there

90

arresting Beecher Block. Every second it takes you morons to do that is another second I have to wait to file suit against him."

"First of all, there is no conclusive proof that Beecher had anything to do with this. I assure you we're doing everything we can to bring the guilty party to justice. You coming down here making a scene isn't going to help us find out who did this any faster, so why don't you turn yourself around, head back home, and wait it out like everyone else?"

Chance didn't bother being polite. Crystal was the type of girl that cared more about money and status than sympathy, so any politeness Chance may have been able to muster up would have been a wasted effort anyway.

"Chance Holleran, I do not care for your tone, and I am not going anywhere until you explain what the hell is going on and why Beecher Block isn't on his way to the electric chair."

Chance looked at Andy and Mike then grinned at them like the Cheshire Cat.

"You know what, you two seem hell-bent on running this investigation without me, so you deal with her."

Chance turned, walked into his office, and slammed the door.

Mike Collins had enjoyed watching Chance take the brunt of Crystal's abuse. It was kind of refreshing to watch her berate someone else for a change. Long before Crystal became Cane Jessop's nightmare, she had been Mike's. Watching her in action now made him grateful that she'd moved on.

"Mike Collins, what are you looking at? Do not be getting any ideas about you and me. Cane ain't even in the ground yet, and I ain't fixing to take up with the likes of you again anyway."

Mike turned bright red, and Andy thought the poor kid might choke on his tongue.

"Crystal, I swear you get bat-shit crazier every time I see you. Cane isn't going to die, so I'm not sure why you think you have any grounds to sue anyone."

"You know full well that I'm carrying his child, and anyone trying to hurt Cane is trying to cheat me out of what is rightfully mine. I have a right to be compensated for the pain and suffering that all this has caused me."

"Your pain and suffering? Give it a rest, Crystal. We both know that the only one suffering in your relationship is Cane."

"You're just bitter, Mike Collins, because Cane had the good sense to make an honest woman out of me."

Crystal did not wait for a reply before storming out the same way she had come in.

As soon as she was gone, Chance reappeared in his office doorway.

"Tell me, Mikey, do you ever wake up in a cold sweat, crawl out of bed, get on your knees, and thank the good Lord above that you're not the object of her affection anymore?"

"I don't even wait until I'm asleep. I never go to bed without thanking the big guy for that save. I just feel sorry that Cane's now tied to her for the next eighteen years."

"I wouldn't be so sure about that, Mikey. From what I hear, Cane has his doubts about whose Y chromosome produced that litter of doom."

"Litter of doom? Seriously, Chance? Everyone in town knows you took your turn with Crystal, so why not have some decency and go a little easy on her? She can't be all bad, considering the way you guys all hound around after her," Andy said.

"Not that bad? You spent enough time diddling her mama back in the day. Take that train wreck and multiply it by two or three hundred, and then tell me if you think she ain't all that bad."

Chance had a point. Bambi Perdix had been Andy's high school sweetheart. She was drop dead gorgeous and had a body that could cause a traffic accident. She was also bossy, controlling, and attracted drama like cow paddies attract flies.

Chance and Mikey spent the next several minutes discussing who might be the father of Crystal's baby. Andy listened carefully, hoping to catch the name of anyone who might want to eliminate the competition.

"I hate to interrupt this riveting dialog between you two but has it occurred to either of you that whoever is the father of Crystal's baby just might have a motive to want Cane out of the way?"

"Like I said earlier, I've got no idea why you're even here, Hansen. I still think Put Newsome was the intended victim and that your soon-to-be brother-in-law is our guy, which means I don't want you anywhere near this investigation. It also means that Mikey is off limits until I make an arrest."

Andy sneered at Chance. "Funny, I recall telling you that Red Dixon needed to stay away from his daughter's investigation yet you couldn't keep your big trap shut and almost sank the whole thing. You can just consider this payback. How's it feel?"

"How would a shock in the ass with my Taser feel? Mikey still has a job and needs to get back to work so I suggest you find something else to do with your afternoon. I hear Burger King over in Bishop has openings. Maybe the girlfriend could teach you how to flip burgers."

"You keep crowing, Chance. I've got a suspension hearing tomorrow with the Council. Once it's over, I promise to remember every arrogant word you've spewed when I kick your ass out of my office and send you back to Red Dixon with your tail between your legs."

"I'm well aware of that, Andy, and Red and I plan to be there to present all the reasons why you don't deserve this badge."

Chance made a show of flicking the golden Sheriff's badge attached to his belt. A badge that Andy used to wear proudly across his heart.

***

After an hour of stuffing their faces, Q'Bita and Rene finally threw in the towel. They were both so full they couldn't breathe, and Rolfie was starting to look bored. They paid the bill then Rene took Rolfie and headed out for more retail reconnaissance, as he liked to call it. They both knew it was more shop and gossip, though. A quick glance at her watch told Q'Bita she'd better head to the Italian market and hightail it home to start prepping for class.

As Q'Bita reached the market, the automatic door swished open and a distracted Mariah Sinclair almost knocked her over.

"Oh, Miss Block, I'm sorry, I wasn't paying attention."

"No worries, and please, call me Q'Bita. How's Henri doing?"

"I have wonderful news, actually. He's awake and talking. It only took him about three sentences to ask when he could have an espresso," Mariah said, holding up the bag of coffee she'd just purchased.

"That's fantastic. I'm so happy for you both. Is he allowed to have visitors yet?"

"Yes. He asked about you, and I'm sure he'd love to see you."

"I have class this evening but let him know that I'll stop by tomorrow.

Mariah said goodbye and Q'Bita made her way inside to pick up her order. She had just paid and was making her way to the door when Hilde Sanders popped up in front of her like a deranged stalker.

"Hello, Q'Bita. I'm so glad I ran into you before class. I hate asking personal questions during class for fear our conversation will end up being spread all over town."

Q'Bita bit her tongue to keep from saying what she was really thinking.

"Hello, Hilde. I'd love to chat with you but I really need to get back to the Red Herring and get things ready for class."

"Oh, I'm sure you do. I'm guessing you're a little short-handed without Evie. She must be devastated. I can't imagine what she must be going through, wondering if Cane will pull through and then knowing that the killer is still out there and might come back to finish the job."

Hilde was in rare form today, and Q'Bita wasn't sure she had the strength to deal with her, but she was a means to an end. If anybody in town had the scoop, it was sure to be Hilde.

"I hear that Cane is doing well. The Newsomes are a strong family, and I'm sure they'll be just fine."

Hilde made a show of looking around before she leaned in closer to Q'Bita.

"How are you holding up, dear? It must be so hard having everyone in town thinking your brother is behind this."

"Actually, I'm just fine. I know my brother, and I assure you, Beecher would never hurt anyone, especially not one of his closest friends."

"Of course not, dear, but rumor has it that Beecher wasn't aiming for Cane."

Q'Bita was starting to lose her patience with Hilde, and it was getting harder to remain polite.

"Beecher wasn't aiming for anyone because Beecher had nothing to do with this. I'm sure this will all get sorted once Chance figures out what really happened."

"Oh my, I appear to have touched a nerve. Not my intention, I assure you. I just hope that everything goes well with Andy's hearing tomorrow, then he can take over the investigation and resolve things quickly."

This last comment caught Q'Bita off guard, and she tried to control her facial expression. Andy hadn't told her that he had a hearing tomorrow but she didn't want Hilde to know that.

"No, you're fine, Hilde. I'm just tired and not quite myself today. I'd love to chat more but I really do need to get back."

"Well then, I guess we can finish our chat this evening. I wouldn't miss this class for anything."

"I'm sure you wouldn't," Q'Bita said as she stepped past Hilde and quickly headed for the door.

As soon as Q'Bita was a safe distance from Hilde, she pulled out her phone and called Andy.

"Hello, beautiful. What's going on?"

"You tell me. I just heard from Hilde Sanders that you have a hearing tomorrow. Why didn't you tell me?"

"I'm sorry, babe. I just found out this morning on my way into town. I was going to tell you as soon as I got home. I promise."

Q'Bita relaxed a little and apologized for sounding upset.

"So why do you think the Council scheduled the hearing on such short notice?"

"I don't know. I wondered the same thing myself. Part of me suspects they're worried Chance can't handle Cane's investigation and they want me to do it, but most of them are run so far up Red's ass that it's got me worried that it could be something else."

"You don't think they've decided to move forward with Red's private policing idea, do you?"

"If they have, they're in for a world of trouble, because I'll spend every last penny I've got suing them for whatever I can. I understand why I got suspended. I crossed the line, and that was wrong, but there's a limit to how far I plan to let this crap go, and I've just about reached it."

"I'm sorry, sweetheart. I know this must be hard on you. Is there anything I can do?"

Andy laughed, and it instantly made her feel better.

"I'll let Kent Haskell do the heavy lifting. You just keep the pie coming, and I'm sure it will all work out just fine."

"I'm headed back to the Red Herring now, so I'll see what I can do about that pie."

"Okay, but you'd better hurry. Your dad will be back soon, and I think he likes pie just as much as I do."

"Andy, no one likes pie as much as you do."

They talked for a few more seconds then Andy's phone beeped and he put her on hold. When he switched back, he told her that it was Clarity Fessler, and he was going to go meet her and Orvis for lunch but would head straight home afterwards so she could tell him what she knew so far.

"What makes you think I know anything?" Q'Bita asked.

"Because I know you, sweetheart, and I'd bet a week's worth of pie that you and the Hardy Boys were on the case the second I walked out the door this morning."

Q'Bita played innocent but knew that Andy saw right through her.

"You enjoy your lunch. I'll talk to you when you get back."

Q'Bita felt a mix of emotions wash over her as she hung up. Part of her was happy that Henri and Cane were doing better but a bigger part of her felt like the worst was far from over.

Chapter 16

Andy could see Clarity and Orvis in a huddle halfway across the diner, and their conversation looked intense. They saw him coming and quickly stopped talking. Andy got the impression they were talking about him.

"Hey, Andy," Orvis said a little too enthusiastically.

"Orvis. Clarity. I hope I didn't interrupt something important."

Clarity glanced down at the table to avoid eye contact. Andy saw Orvis shake his head.

"Why don't you have a seat and we'll order, then we can talk shop," Orvis suggested.

Andy pulled out the chair across from Clarity, who was now pretending to be engrossed in the menu.

"I sense some tension. Am I even going to want to eat after I hear what you have to say?"

Andy heard Clarity stifle a small sob behind the menu and knew he wasn't imagining that something was wrong. Clarity wasn't the emotional type, so whatever had upset her this much, it couldn't be good news.

Clarity put down the menu and looked up at Andy. Her eyes were puffy and red and her lower lip was trembling.

"Andy, I'm so sorry. I've been over the evidence three times, and each time it all pointed to Beecher Block. I swear to you I tried to find something, anything, that would point to someone else but there just isn't anything."

"Okay, tell me what you have so far."

Clarity grabbed a napkin and blew her nose then launched into a detailed explanation of the evidence.

"The footprints at the scene are from a set of size eleven Irish Setter 808 Wingshooter waterproof nine-inch upland hunting boots with something about the size of a pea lodged in the second row of the tread on the right foot. I know Beecher wears this brand. I've seen them. Then there's the crossbow bolt. It was pretty high-end stuff, custom-made. I traced it back to the manufacturer in Orem Utah and spoke to the Customer Service Manager, who confirmed who placed the order."

"Why do I have a feeling I already know the answer?"

"According to their shipping records, the order was placed by Rene Block and delivered with a special message for his husband regarding their anniversary."

Andy was quiet for a few seconds while he contemplated everything he'd just heard.

"Andy, I know you know this but I'm going to say it anyway. Everything Clarity's just shared with you absolutely cannot leave this table. I have some additional information and I'm more than willing to share it with you but you have to promise me that you'll keep it under wraps until Chance decides what to do with it."

"Ya, I hear you, Orvis. Doesn't mean I like it, but I hear you. Chance may be sitting in my office and driving my SUV but until the Council serves me my pink slip, I'm still the actual Sherriff and I know better than to do anything else that might jeopardize that."

"Even if that means keeping a secret from your girlfriend?" Clarity asked quietly.

Andy suddenly lost his appetite. He and Q'Bita didn't keep secrets, and she was sure to ask what Clarity and Orvis knew about the case. If he told her the truth and she reacted badly, then he might never get his job back. On the other hand, if he held back and she found out later that he'd kept this from her, he just might lose her. As much as he loved being the Castle Creek Sherriff, he loved her more. He just hoped Clarity and Orvis couldn't see that he was lying to them."

"I guess I'll just have to roll the dice and hope that Q'Bita will understand."

Orvis gave him a wary look then shared that the trajectory of the entry wound matched the footprint evidence and that whoever took the shot would have to be an experienced hunter or archer to have hit Cane."

"Okay, so what distance were the footprints from where Cane was hit?" Andy asked.

"Exactly forty-eight yards," Clarity said.

"Do you get a report on wind speed from the NWS?" Andy asked.

Clarity gave him and odd look and Andy saw the expression on

Orvis's face change from serious to curious.

"No, I didn't, but it was beautiful out so I don't think weather would have been much of a factor," Clarity said.

"Actually, Clarity, Andy's right, and I think I know where he's going with this," Orvis said.

"It was hot and humid as hell that day, which has a big impact on a bow. When a bow heats up it expands, which can throw off its normal adjustments, and the humidity changes the density of the air, which results in less drag on the bolt as it passes through the air," Andy explained.

"Okay, so what does that have to do with the evidence?" Clarity asked.

"It means that Chance is going to have a hell of a time making a case against Beecher," Orvis said.

"Sorry, I still don't understand."

"What Orvis is trying to say, Clarity, is that your evidence presents a motive problem. Beecher is the most experienced bow hunter in Castle Creek. He would know how the heat and humidity would affect his equipment and the bolt flight and would have made the necessary adjustments if he was trying to hit Put. Beecher has zero motive to want to hurt Cane."

"But they were dressed identically. From a distance, no one would have been able to tell them apart."

"Almost identically. Their caps were different, and Put's pants were too short," Orvis corrected.

"Yep, and if someone with Beecher's hunting skills were planning on killing Put, he wouldn't have missed details like that, especially if he knew he was going to have to tell them apart later."

Andy noticed a change in Clarity's posture that almost looked defensive, and her tone was sharp when she spoke.

"I can't believe I missed that. I was sure I did everything right."

"Hey, don't be so hard on yourself, Clarity. I'm not saying your findings are flawed. I'm sure they're spot-on. I'm just saying that rather than implicating Beecher, they support the fact that it may have been someone else."

Orvis used the arrival of their food as an opportunity to change the subject to something less work-related. They ate quickly, and Clarity paid her bill then excused herself as soon as they'd finished.

After she left, Andy turned to Orvis. "Was it just me or did she seem really out of sorts? I didn't mean to upset her."

"I wouldn't take it too personally, Andy. She's been dealing with a lot lately. She told me recently that her mother hasn't been doing well since Clarity's father passed, and things have escalated recently. She feels guilty for not being there for her mother but I gather that there are some expenses associated with his death and she needs to keep working."

"Wow, I'm sorry to hear that. It's hard enough to deal with something like that when you're an adult but she's still just a kid."

"Well, since I have you here, there's something I want you to hear from me before it just gets sprung on you," Orvis said.

"Sure, why not? This day just keeps getting better and better. Might as well toss a grenade into the mix."

Orvis gave him a pained look and shook his head.

"About this hearing tomorrow. I wanted you to know that the Council made an official request for release of all the information my office had on Cane's case. That includes everything Clarity shared with you. I have no idea what their end game is, Andy, but I felt you should be aware of it before you walk in there tomorrow. I also want you to know that I don't think for one second that Beecher had anything to do with this, and if I wasn't legally obligated to hand it over, I wouldn't give them anything."

"I appreciate you giving me the heads-up, Orvis. I'm not sure what they're up to either, but if I had to guess, I'd say Red Dixon has more than a small hand in it."

"All the more reason to tread carefully. You still have friends on the Council, so go in there and convince the rest of them that you're still the best man for the job. Just do it by the book and don't let your temper get the best of you."

***

By the time Q'Bita reached the Red Herring, her nana had already returned from picking up her parents. Q'Bita pulled into the side drive and found her mother picking some basil from the kitchen garden. When her mother saw her, she dropped her basket and rushed toward her with arms wide open.

"Oh baby, I'm so sorry we weren't here when you needed us. I promise we won't leave again until everything gets back to normal around here."

Q'Bita loved her mother's hugs. They were the kind that practically smothered you, and it was exactly what she needed this week.

After an extra strong squeeze, her mother let go and stepped back to look at her.

"Be honest, Q'Bita, how are you doing? I'm sure the shock of finding out Alain is still alive must have been overwhelming."

"Actually, I'm doing great. I punched him in the face and broke his nose. It was cathartic."

"That's my girl."

"The Alain situation is under control for now. He should be leaving in a day or two. Now if we could just solve Beecher's problem, you might be able to get back to your book tour."

"The tour can wait. Besides, there's been a change of plans regarding the series, so your father and I will be staying put for a while. I do have to say, this never would have happened if Andy were still Sheriff."

"I agree. Hopefully, his suspension hearing will go his way tomorrow... but he's worried, for sure."

Her mother sighed. "Castle Creek used to be such a nice little town but lately it's like the whole town's gone crazy."

Q'Bita was cut off mid-reply by the sound of crunching gravel. She turned to see Alain's rental car entering the driveway.

"Oh crap. I do not have the patience to deal with him right now," she muttered.

"Is that—"

"Yes, it's Alain. You have my permission to berate him full-force."

"Can I re-break his nose?"

"Be my guest."

Alain pulled to stop a few feet away and got out of the car.

"Ladies, always a pleasure to see you both."

"Your charm will get you nowhere with either one of us, Alain La Roche. I have half a mind to kick your pasty butt all the way back to France."

"Kari, I don't know what Q'Bita has told you but I have a perfectly reasonable explanation for what occurred. She simply refuses to listen to reason and instead has chosen to resort to violence and pettiness."

Q'Bita turned to her mother and smiled. "I forgot to mention that I have moved Alain's accommodations to the loft."

"Since when do we have a loft?"

"We've always had one. It's in the main barn, above the old stalls. I made sure he had fresh linens and asked Jamie to leave chocolates on his pillow."

Alain wrinkled his face in disgust. "Yes, as I said, pettiness."

Kari snorted out loud then doubled over laughing.

Q'Bita could tell from the look on his face that Alain was not amused.

"Well, this conversation has been enlightening, to say the least. It's now apparent to me where your manners come from, Q'Bita."

Alain turned, got back in his car, and drove off without saying anything else.

"Gee, do you think it was something we said?" her mother asked then started laughing all over again.

Q'Bita grabbed the baguettes and meat from the car as her mother finished picking herbs. Her nana was already in the kitchen, prepping for class.

"Ah, wonderful. I hope you brought an extra loaf or two of that for sampling. I'm old; I have to keep my strength up."

Q'Bita set her bags on the counter and gave her nana a quick peck on the cheek.

"I have something in these bags that I think you'll like even better."

"Child, please tell me that it's Rose's honey lavender madeleines."

Q'Bita plated the pillowy, delicious treats and set them next to her nana. Liddy Lou downed three of them before Q'Bita returned with the lemonade.

"Wow, Rose was right. You really do like those," Q'Bita teased.

"What can I say? I'm a stress eater. Now grab yourself one or two before I eat them all, and help me get this prep work done."

When Andy arrived back home, she grabbed him a huge slice of lemon tart and they took a break on the porch.

"So you and the Scooby Gang uncover any clues?"

"Mock me if you want but you know darn well that I and my team have been very useful when it comes to solving crime around here."

"Oh, so you have a team now, do you?" Andy laughed.

"I do, and if you promise to play nice, I might let you join my team."

"Depending on how this hearing goes tomorrow, I might need to take you up on that."

"I refuse to believe that the Council is foolish enough to let that happen. Even they have to know that Chance is a joke and that letting Red Dixon run local law enforcement is just asking for trouble."

Q'Bita noticed that Andy had hardly touched his pie.

"Is there something wrong with the pie?"

"No, just not really all that hungry, I guess."

Q'Bita reached over and felt his forehead with the back of her hand.

"You felling okay?"

"Ya, just a lot on my mind, I guess."

"Anything I can help with?"

"Depends. How close are you guys to figuring out who really shot that arrow?"

Q'Bita spent the next few minutes telling Andy everything she and Rene had learned so far. When she was finished, he shared what had happened at the station with Crystal Perdix. He was just about finished when Liddy Lou joined them on the porch. She took a long sip of lemonade and proceeded to put her two cents in.

"Now y'all didn't hear this from me, because I don't spread gossip, but Chance is right about Cane having doubts. I have it on very good authority that he's already broken things off with Crystal and asked for a paternity test when the child is born. Crystal did not take this well and has been pitching a fit from here to Bishop since it happened."

"Interesting. This authority of yours have any plans to share this with Chance?" Andy asked.

"I think my source would rather wait and see what happens with your hearing tomorrow."

Andy jabbed at the pie with his folk and then pushed the plate away.

"Well, I just hope y'all don't end up disappointed. Now if you ladies will excuse me, I guess I'd better go give Kent Haskell a call about tomorrow."

***

Even though the class had been full, Q'Bita didn't really learn anything new or useful. There was some chittering about Cane and Crystal's breakup, and some whispering that Chance or Mike Collins might be the father of Crystal's child, but Q'Bita chalked most of that up to speculation.

By the time they'd cleaned up and she got upstairs, Andy was sound asleep on the couch and Allegro was curled up in a ball on his chest, snoring almost as loudly as Andy. She made it all the way to the kitchen without waking either of them but Allegro woke up and yipped when she opened the fridge.

"Hey, Q'Bita. Sorry, I didn't hear you come in. What time is it?"

"Time to take this little fur ball out for a potty break. I brought you a sandwich and some lemon cream pie just in case your appetite returned."

"Have I ever told you that I love you? I could eat a horse right about now."

Andy handed her Allegro, and he immediately started licking her chin.

"Okay, mister, let's get you outside before you sprinkle the front of my shirt with liquid joy."

Andy gave her a raised eyebrow and then shook his head.

"You two have a bond I definitely do not understand."

"Go eat your dinner. We'll be right back."

As they made their way down the hall, Q'Bita snapped the leash on Allegro's collar and sat him down to walk beside her. He immediately started growling and pulling on the leash. She turned to see Alain coming down the hall toward her.

"Quite the guard dog you have there. You'd think he'd respond a little nicer, considering I'm the reason he's staying with you."

"I guess it's true what they say about dogs being excellent judges of character."

"Q'Bita, don't you find this continuous barrage of insults exhausting? I know I certainly do."

"I find you exhausting. The insults are mostly for my own entertainment. Now, what do you want?"

"I came to speak to you about my accommodations. I think I've been punished sufficiently and would like to be moved back inside."

"Sorry, we're still fully booked. You're welcome to look for a room somewhere else, and I'll have Jamie refund the charge for your unused days."

"I would think you'd want me here, considering that there may well be a killer still wandering around out there."

"I don't need you to protect me, Alain. I have Andy for that."

Alain scowled. "Yes, I suppose so, but unlike Andrew, I still have a career in law enforcement. Speaking of that, I do hope everything goes well with his hearing tomorrow."

His scowl was now replaced with a smirk as he turned and walked back down the hall in the direction he'd come from.

His tone left Q'Bita with an uneasy feeling and a suspicion that there was a hint of something brewing behind his comment.

***

Neither Q'Bita nor Andy had slept well, and morning came way too soon. Q'Bita did her best to keep Andy's mind off his hearing while they had their coffee and breakfast but she could see it wasn't working.

"Andy, I know you said I should stay here but I really think I should go with you. You're a little distracted, and I'm worried about you."

"Okay, but I can't promise you that I'll be the best company. This whole thing is just eating at me, and I can't say I'm going to be able to keep calm if it doesn't go my way."

"I understand, and that's just one more reason why I think I should be there."

Andy didn't say much on the drive into town, and Q'Bita decided it was best to just let him sit with his thoughts. When they got to City Hall, the small parking lot was almost full, and Andy let loose a cuss word or two.

"Looks like they decided to have a little pre-hearing pow-wow without me. I don't like the thought of that."

Q'Bita put a hand on his shoulder and gave it a squeeze. Andy turned toward her and gave her a small smile.

"Andy, I hope you know that no matter what happens in there today, I love you, and nothing can change that. I'm going to be right be your side no matter where that takes us."

He reached up, wrapped her tiny hand in his and gave it a kiss.

"I know, Q'Bita, and that's the only thing keeping me going right now."

Q'Bita looked up and noticed the WCMP news van pulling into the parking lot.

"Crap. Spenser's here. You go in. I'll distract him."

"I love that you're willing to sacrifice yourself for me, babe. Remind me to leave you a slice of pie when we get home."

Q'Bita planted a quick peck on his check as Andy hopped out of the car and bolted for the doors. Spenser was out of the van and running to catch up before the news van had even come to a full stop. Q'Bita waited for her opening and threw open the door to block his path. Spenser skidded to a stop, almost toppling over.

"Miss Block, that was neither necessary nor appreciated. We have freedom of the press in this country, and you cannot stop me from doing my job."

Q'Bita stepped out of the car and nudged Spenser back a few steps. "I have no idea what you're talking about, Spenser. I just opened my door, and there you were."

Q'Bita glanced over her shoulder to make sure Andy had made it inside then closed her car door. "Sorry, Spenser, I'd love to stay and chat but I need to get inside. The hearing is about to start."

Q'Bita walked away, leaving Spenser staring at her back side. Once she got inside, she was surprised to see Andy's Aunt Maggie sitting alone on a bench just outside the Council chambers.

"Hello, Maggie. I wasn't expecting to see you here. How are you doing?"

Maggie stood and gave her a huge hug.

"Oh, Q'Bita, I'm so glad to see you. Can you believe that Red and Chance had the audacity to have me listed as a witness for their side? If this was a real court and not a circus, I'd definitely have to be listed as a hostile witness. I've got no idea what those two are playing at but I'll tell you this much, they'd better not call me or I'll tell them exactly what I think of this horse-and-pony show."

"I kind of hope they do call you, Maggie. Andy needs someone in his corner in there."

They took a seat on the bench and waited. Q'Bita could hear the occasional raised voice but she couldn't hear what was being said, and it seemed like time had stopped moving. An hour later the doors burst open and Andy came storming out, with Alain right behind him.

They stopped in front of Maggie and Q'Bita, and Andy whirled on Alain.

"You listen to me, you maggot, you think this man you've been running from is dangerous? You haven't seen anything yet. You've crossed a line that you ain't gonna be able to uncross, and this isn't over. When I'm finished with you, there isn't gonna be anything left for your enemies to come after."

Alain flinched but otherwise remained the picture of smug composure. Rather than address Andy directly, he turned toward her.

"Can you honestly tell me that this surly, ill-tempered Neanderthal is the person you want to spend the rest of your life with? You can do better than that. Actually, you have done better than that, considering we're still married."

Q'Bita didn't waste a second jumping between the two. She wasn't going to take any chances that Andy might sock Alain.

"Alain, what the hell are you doing here?"

"The Council was aware of my law-enforcement expertise and engaged me as a consultant."

"Bullshit! You threw in with Red and Chance, thinking you could force me into a decision that either leaves Chance as Sheriff or damages my relationship with Q'Bita. Either way I'm screwed, but you aren't going to get away with this."

Q'Bita held up a hand to silence them both.

"Andy, what are you talking about? What happened in there?"

"This jack hole convinced the Council to reinstate me but only if I agree to arrest Beecher."

Q'Bita took a step back and looked at them both.

"You can't be serious," she said.

"I feel as though Andrew may have misconstrued my intent. I simply felt that if he really wanted his position back, then he should demonstrate a small amount of good faith and prove that, going forward, he won't let his personal emotions dictate his actions as Sheriff. His accusation that I did this for personal gain just shows me that he's ill-equipped for the role."

"I'm about to show you what a good old-fashioned ass-whooping looks like."

"Careful, Andrew. If I'm not mistaken, it was your penchant for physical violence that got you in this mess in the first place, was it not?"

Q'Bita had heard enough.

"Alain, you need to shut up right now before I deck you again myself. If you thought for one second that this was going to cause tension between me and Andy, you're an idiot. Did it ever occur to you that given the choice between Andy arresting Beecher and then being the one to conduct the investigation or leaving Beecher's fate in the hands of Chance and Red Dixon, I just might be okay with Andy doing what he had to do?"

The look of horror on Alain's face was priceless. The look on Andy's face told her that she was definitely going to spend the rest of her life with the right man.

"Q'Bita, are you sure? They aren't going to give me my job back if I don't arrest your brother. We both know he didn't do this, and I don't want this job back bad enough to do that to him or to you."

"Andy, I'm sure. The fact that you believe Beecher is exactly why I want you to do this. You're Beecher's only chance for a fair investigation."

Andy pulled her close and gave her a kiss so amazing it made her knees buckle.

"I love you, babe. I promise I won't let you down."

Alain had turned pale and Q'Bita could see by the bulge in his jaw that he was gritting his teeth.

She'd almost forgotten Maggie was still there until she appeared beside Andy.

"I have no idea who you are but I think you're done here. This is a family matter, and we'll resolve it as a family."

Andy bent down and kissed the top of his aunt's head.

"Does this mean you're coming back to work?"

"You just tell me what time you want me there and I'll be there with bells on."

Andy wrapped them both in a hug and held them tight for a few seconds. He whispered thank you to them both and then let go.

"Okay, I guess I'd better get in there and give them my decision."

When Q'Bita turned around, Alain was gone.

Andy had only been inside a few minutes when Chance and Red came through the door.

"Damn it, Red, you and Frenchie guaranteed me that Andy would never take the bait."

Chance stopped talking as soon as he saw Q'Bita and Maggie.

Q'Bita stepped in front of them and looked directly at Chance.

"Did I just hear you say that Red and Alain knew in advance that they were going to put Andy in this position?"

Chance started to speak but Red interrupted him. "I understand how upsetting this must be for you, Q'Bita. Knowing that your fiancé just chose his job over your family has to sting. But you have this all wrong. My only motivation was to provide Castle Creek with the best version of law enforcement possible. As for your husband, I'd say he was just trying to protect you from yourself. In hindsight, it appears that we underestimated just how far Hansen was willing to go to get his job back, but desperate men often do surprising things. I'm not too worried, though. I'm sure things will be set right when Chance wins the election."

Q'Bita was getting ready to unload on Red with both barrels when Maggie grasped her arm and tugged on her.

"Come on, Q'Bita. These piss ants aren't worth the breath it would take to tell them off. Let's get Andy and get out of here. The stench of swine is starting to make my eyes water."

Chapter 17

On the ride back to the Red Herring Inn, the reality of the situation finally sank in and Q'Bita's stomach was in knots. She hoped that Andy and Kent Haskell were right and that arresting Beecher would just be a formality.

Q'Bita pulled into the Red Herring Inn and saw Beecher and Rene waiting for her on the porch. She stayed in her car for a minute and took several deep breaths, trying to calm herself. She took one final inhale and braced herself for what was sure to be a very difficult conversation.

Rene darted off the porch like Rolfie pouncing on a bird in the garden. She had no idea how he could walk so fast in wedge heels.

"Q'Bita, how could you let this happen?"

Rene was shouting and overemphasizing every syllable. He was wearing bright yellow pedal-pushers and a low-cut yellow and lapis striped blouse with princess sleeves that fluttered behind him like wings as he stalked toward her.

"I am not letting Andy Hansen drag Beecher off to jail like some common criminal just so he can get his little tin brooch back."

"Rene, heel," Beecher yelled from the porch.

Rene stopped and executed a half-turn worthy of a ballerina.

"Do not address me like one of your hunting hounds while you stand there acting like everything will be okay. Everything is most certainly not okay, Beecher, and if you are not going to protect yourself, I am going to intervene on your behalf and take charge."

Rene turned back around and was about to start in on her again when Andy and Kent Haskell pulled into the driveway.

"You wait here, Q'Bita. I'm not finished with you yet but I have bigger fish to deal with right now."

Q'Bita watched as Rene marched up to Andy and shoved both of his hands in Andy's face.

"You might as well just slap a pair of cuffs on my wrists right now because I have no intention of letting you, or anyone else, take my husband. I am fully prepared to strip off naked, tie myself to the grille of this SUV, and stage a hunger strike if that's what it takes to stop you."

Q'Bita was positive that Rene meant every word and if someone didn't do something quick they were all about to see more of Rene than most of them ever wanted to see. Fortunately, Beecher knew just how to deal with his husband.

"Rene, if you don't come back up here, fully clothed, right now, I swear to you I will cancel every credit card we have and stop automatic shipping on your Pumps of The Month Club."

Rene gasped and put his left hand to his breast in mock horror while fanning himself with his right hand.

"Do you people see what you've done? He's not even in jail yet and he's already cracked under the stress. No sane man would ever say such hurtful things to the one he loves. You've ruined him."

Q'Bita could see that Andy was really trying hard to be civil but she wasn't sure how much longer he could hold out.

"Rene, I need you to take a battery out for a while so Kent and I can discuss this with Beecher. You have my word that I will clear Beecher, but I'm going to need everyone's help, and that includes you."

Rene threw his hands up in frustration and sauntered back to the porch. Q'Bita, Andy, and Kent joined them on the porch. As they reached the front door, Rene stopped and gave Q'Bita a look that would have wilted most people.

"You had just better hope that this all turns out okay because, as of now, you're dead to me, and the only way this friendship is going to be resurrected is if that traitor fiancé of yours clears Beecher's good name. Even then you're going to have to work your pretty little backside off to earn back my trust. You've wounded me to the core and I will not soon forgive you."

Rene dismissed her with a flick of his hand and walked inside. Beecher put his arm around her and pulled her close.

"Q'Bita, don't worry about Rene. He didn't mean what he said. He'll be fine in a few hours."

Q'Bita felt tears welling in her eyes. "Actually, Beecher, I'm not so sure about that, and quite honestly, I have no idea why you aren't furious with me too."

"Because I love you and I know that you've always had my back. I'm not stupid, Q'Bita. I know that Chance Holleran would have thrown me in jail and called it a day. You were right to tell Andy to take his job back. He's good at his job, and with him, you, and Jamie on the case, I've got nothing to worry about."

***

After what felt like an eternity, the guys emerged from the library and Q'Bita was happy to see that Beecher was not in cuffs. Andy had agreed to allow Beecher to turn himself in at 9 a.m. the following morning. They'd process him on a charge of reckless endangerment, and then Andy and Kent would speak to Judge Tanner about having Beecher released on his own recognizance.

By the time everyone left Andy looked exhausted, and Q'Bita just wanted to hug him and never let go but she knew that pie would be a much greater comfort to him right now.

"Hey, handsome, I've got something in the walk-in I think might cheer you up."

"I'm not sure if I deserve pie right now, babe. I knew this was going to be tough, but I'm worried that I did some damage with your family."

Q'Bita heard footsteps behind her. Her father had snuck up on them without a sound.

"Rene will be fine eventually. As for the rest of us, we plan to give you the benefit of the doubt."

"Hi, Daddy."

Q'Bita's father flashed them a smile that could melt an iceberg with its warmth.

"Any chance you have enough pie for your old man to join you?"

Andy and her father exchanged small talk while she popped a sour cream pear pie into the warmer and grabbed some bourbon brown sugar ice cream for the top. It sounded like the perfect comfort food combination for a day like today.

By the time she made her way back to the kitchen her mother had joined them too. She helped Q'Bita put the finishing touches on the dessert. Everyone was too busy eating to say much at first but Q'Bita saw her parents having one of their silent conversations. She had never figured out how they did it but her parents could hold a complete conversation using just facial expressions.

"Something you two want to share with us?" Q'Bita asked.

"Actually, there is. I think we could all use some good news right about now."

"I'd second that," Andy said.

"Kari, you want to do the honors?"

Her mother lit up like a Roman candle on the Fourth of July.

"Oh, this is so exciting. I've been dying to tell you all. While we were on the book tour we got a call from an old friend in Hollywood. He'd read Smuggler's Blues and loved it. He flew up to Seattle to meet us for dinner and offered us a deal."

"Congratulations! That's fantastic," Q'Bita said.

Andy nodded and took another big bite of pie.

"I haven't even gotten to the best part yet so hold on to your stools. The offer wasn't just for the movie rights to Smuggler's Blues. He wants the rights to all five books."

Kari squealed and clapped her hands like a kid at a puppet show.

"Wow, my pap would be impressed. I'm sorry he isn't here to see this," Andy said.

Q'Bita watched as her parents exchanged glances again. She wasn't sure what, but she sensed that there was more to this news.

"I'm sorry too, Andy. Jock was a good man and a good friend. I miss him every day. That's why we want to include you and Maggie in this," her father said.

Andy stopped mid-bite and looked at her parents.

"I'm not sure I follow you, Tom."

"What Tom's trying to say is that we aren't going to move forward with any of this unless you and Maggie are on board. This series is based on the stories your grandfather shared with us, and we wouldn't feel right making a deal that didn't include Jock's family."

"Excuse my ignorance but I have no idea how any of this works. When you say 'deal', what does that involve?" Andy asked.

Tom and Kari looked at each other and chuckled.

"Deal means they want it bad enough to pay extremely well for it."

"How many zeros are in extremely?"

"If we play our cards right, I wouldn't be surprised if we can get five or six of those."

Andy made a chocking noise and Q'Bita jumped.

"You're joking, right?"

"Tom never jokes about money."

"I can't speak for Maggie, but I'm definitely in. Where do I sign?"

"Well, let's talk to Maggie, and if she's okay with everything, then we can set up a meeting with our agent. He can go over all the details, and if everyone agrees, he'll handle the negotiations. Once he's gotten an offer we're all happy with, then we can sign the paperwork."

Andy looked at her with a huge grin. "How much pie do you think that kind of money can buy?"

"You could buy your own bakery for that kind of money, sweetheart."

"I could, but it wouldn't be as good as your pie, babe."

Q'Bita sat back and listened as Andy and her parents continued to discuss the finer points of big deals. Eventually, the conversation turned more serious as Andy explained how he and Kent planned to handle Beecher's situation. She was relieved that her parents were keeping an open mind and placing their trust in Andy. She just wished Rene hadn't taken things so personally. Even though he could be a pain in the ass at times, she loved him dearly and wasn't sure what life would be like without him.

By the time they'd finished talking, Andy and her father had polished off the rest of the pie. Andy headed back to the station to reclaim his office, and her parents snuck off to finish their current work in progress. Q'Bita sat still and enjoyed the silence of the kitchen for a few minutes and then decided to head into town to visit Henri at the hospital.

***

Henri was awake when she arrived and greeted her with an enthusiastic, "Bon jour, mon amie."

Q'Bita gave him a gentle hug and took the chair next to the bed.

"Ah, Q'Bita, the trouble I've caused by asking you to call my boss. You must know, I had no idea. Never once did he tell me the truth. I feel betrayed and foolish for what I've put you through."

"It's okay, Henri. You saved my life, and Jamie's too. That tells me all

I need to know about you as a person. I've also come to realize just how manipulative Alain can be, so I have no trouble believing that he used you for his own personal gain. I'm just glad you're going to be okay."

"My wife tells me you've been very kind to her. I thank you for that."

"You wife is lovely, and she is welcome at the Red Herring Inn for as long as she needs to be here."

They chatted for a while longer, then Henri grew serious.

"So what will happen with Gianni and his men?"

"Gianni took a plea deal. He agreed to tell Chance everything he knew about Carter and Lyle killing Jock and to help Alain find this mystery man he's been running from. After that, Gianni will go into witness protection. His men are in jail and will be prosecuted."

"I do not know if you were brave or foolish to be in the warehouse, Q'Bita, but I am glad you and your friends are safe."

"Depending on who you ask, I'm a bit of both."

This made Henri laugh, which triggered a coughing fit. Q'Bita got him a glass a water and helped fix his pillows. Once he was settled, she filled him in on everything going on with Alain and the situation with Cane Jessop. When she was done Henri let out a long sigh.

"I would never have guessed that so much excitement happens here. I think I will find Lyon quite boring when we must return."

"You could always stay. Castle Creek is a nice place."

"Do not let my wife hear you say that. She has fallen in love with your little town and would move here tomorrow if we could. She is already pestering me to move out of the city so she can have a kitchen garden like yours."

"Well, just know that you will always be welcome here."

Henri yawned and Q'Bita realized that she should let him get some rest. She refilled his water glass and gave him another small hug before leaving.

She checked her phone on the way to her car and saw a missed call form Andy, but no message, so she gave him a call back.

"Hello, beautiful. How's my favorite girl?"

"Well, someone's in a good mood."

"Hard to be in a bad mood when I have my badge back and a multi-movie deal in progress. Only thing better would be a slice of pie and a pretty girl to share it with."

"I'll see what I can do about that, Sheriff. What time do you think you'll be home?"

"I'm almost finished with the paperwork for Judge Tanner then I need to stop over and see Kent, but I should be there in an hour or two."

"Any special requests for dinner?"

"Just me, you, and a little bit of alone time."

"Sounds wonderful."

"I have an even better idea. Why don't you hang around town, or come over here until I'm done, then we can hit Lil's for dinner?"

Lil's was Q'Bita's favorite restaurant and Andy knew she couldn't resist their fried catfish and creamy coleslaw.

"It's a date. I'm going to stop by Sammie Hake's and send Rene some flowers to see if I can smooth things over a little, then I'll come to the station."

"Good idea but you might want to stop by Rose's, too, and send him some of those fancy cookie things he likes."

"Oh, great idea."

Q'Bita hung up and went to Rose's first. She ordered two dozen baci di dama and two dozen anginetti. She then went a few doors down to the florist and had Sammie send a dozen blush pink and cream Peace roses. Sammie and Rose shared the same delivery boy so she arranged to have them delivered together along with a card that said, "I'm sorry I hurt you. Love, Q."

She decided to leave her car where it was and walk the rest of the way to the station. She was almost there when she heard Hilde Sanders calling her name.

"Q'Bita, wait up. I need to talk to you."

She thought about ignoring Hilde but she knew it was no use; Hilde would eventually show up at the station, and Andy didn't need the town crier snooping around on his first day back.

"Hello, Hilde."

"My goodness, you walk fast. I've been trying to chase you down for half a block. Where are you off to in such a hurry?"

Q'Bita ignored the question and asked, "What can I do for you, Hilde?"

Hilde waddled a few steps closer then stopped and bent over to catch her breath.

"I heard that Andy has been reinstated and I have some inside scoop that I think you might want to share with him. It's about Crystal and Cane."

Q'Bita tried not to look too anxious but for once she actually wanted to hear what Hilde had to say.

"I was at Fay's, getting my weekly tease-out, and Dot Nichols was getting that ridiculous up-do that she insists on wearing. I tell you, she looks like one of those 70's sitcom waitresses."

Q'Bita was getting antsy waiting to hear about Crystal and Cane so she decided to hurry things along.

"Hilde, focus. What were you going to tell me about Crystal and Cane?"

"Oh yes. Well, Dot's ex-husband's sister is married to Bob Franklin."

"The financial planner for Castle Creek Savings and Loan?" Q'Bita asked.

"Yes, him. His wife told Dot that Crystal was in last week, asking Bob all kinds of questions about how life insurance policies pay out and how quickly after someone passes away can the beneficiary collect the funds. I thought that sounded like something Andy might want to know."

"I'm sure you're right. Thank you for sharing, Hilde."

"No problem. As much as I hate to gossip, I just couldn't keep something like that to myself. It just wouldn't be right."

Q'Bita was preoccupied, trying to figure out how to extract herself from Hilde, when her phone rang. She pulled it from her pocket and saw that it was Jamie.

"I'm sorry, Hilde, I have to take this call. Let's catch up later."

Q'Bita turned and walked far enough away that Hilde couldn't hear her conversation before answering.

"Hey, Jamie."

"Took you long enough to answer. Hope I'm not interrupting anything inappropriate between you and the man with the badge."

"Lord, no. You actually just saved me from Hilde Sanders."

"What are besties for? Did she have any juicy gossip?"

"She did, but you obviously called for a reason, so let's do you first."

"I hit pay dirt on the alleged Bigfoot footage. My buddy asked around and found the guy that Hank Morgan paid to doctor the tape. The original footage is from one of Hank's trail cams, and it's a black bear walking on his hind legs. Hank paid the guy $2500 to doctor it so the guy didn't ask any questions. "

"So Cane was right. It was fake."

"Here's the best part: I did a little deep-dive on our footage-faker and found out he spends a fortune at Cane's bookstore. I'm guessing that's how Cane found out about the footage being a fake."

"Nice work, Jamie. This is exactly the kind of thing that proves someone other than Beecher had motive."

Q'Bita then took a minute to tell Jamie what Hilde had shared with her.

"Wow, sounds like we both found possible suspects. That has to be something, right?"

"I sure hope so. I'm on my way to the station now. I'll fill Andy in and keep my fingers crossed that this helps when he and Kent talk to Judge Tanner tomorrow.

When she finally reached the station Andy was on the phone, so she walked out to the front lobby intending to write Maggie a welcome-back note, but just as she reached Maggie desk, the front door opened and Bambi Perdix walked in.

Bambi took one look at her and wrinkled her nose.

"Hello, Q'Bita. I'd say I'm surprised to see you here but I'm not. I hear you and Andy are basically inseparable these days. A little clingy if you ask me. Of course, I never worried that he'd stray so I didn't bother keeping him on a leash."

Bambi never missed a chance to throw her past relationship with Andy in Q'Bita's face. It was as predictable as a rooster crowing at the rising sun. At first it really bothered Q'Bita but after a while she realized that Andy wasn't complicated. If he'd wanted Bambi in his life he would have kept her. The fact that he hadn't meant he'd moved on. If Bambi had been the right woman for Andy, she too would have realized this, but the point seemed completely lost on her.

"What can I do for you, Bambi?"

Bambi looked her up and down, and Q'Bita saw her mouth drop open when she spotted the engagement ring. Q'Bita knew it was a childish thing to do but she couldn't stop herself from shoving her left hand forward and turning her wrist back in forth so the light picked up the sparkle.

"Isn't it beautiful? I just love how it catches the light."

Bambi's nose crinkled like she'd just caught a whiff of manure. Her eyes narrowed and she tossed her long red hair back with one hand.

"A little small for my taste but I'm sure it was the best Andy could do on a public servant salary."

"Actually, it was his grandmother's ring. He offered to buy me my own but this one just felt more special, like a sincere gift from the heart."

Q'Bita hated being petty but she took a tiny bit of joy in seeing that this was getting Bambi's goat.

"How sweet. On the bright side, at least you won't have to worry working off those extra pounds you're carrying to fit into a wedding gown. Most brides don't bother with the traditional white gown when it's their second wedding."

As a general rule, Q'Bita tried to never sink to Bambi's level, but calling her fat had gone too far. She channeled her inner Rene and returned Bambi's snark full-blast.

"Wow, for someone who's been through a trailer park full of men but never managed to snag one permanently, you sure seem to be full of wedding advice."

"Okay, ladies, let's woo up for a minute with the verbal sparring."

Q'Bita turned to see Andy standing in the hallway looking at her like she was about to be scolded.

Bambi waltzed past her and stopped directly in front of Andy. She made a show of pushing her large breast outward and sucking in her rounding middle.

"I certainly hope your children end up getting their manners from you and not her."

Andy just shook his head and ignored her comment.

"Is there something I can help you with, Bambi? I'm getting ready to close up shop for the day."

"You can tell me when you plan to arrest Beecher Block. The sooner he's been charged the sooner my Crystal can collect her damages."

Andy leaned against the wall and Q'Bita noticed how tired he looked.

"Listen, Bambi. I get that Crystal is upset, but this crazy idea she has about suing Beecher for pain and suffering is ridiculous. That's not how things work, and she'll just be wasting her time and money on a lawyer who isn't going to get her anything but embarrassment."

"If I didn't know better, I'd say you're just trying to protect your soon-to-be family. You're the Sheriff of this town, and you have to do what's right and ethical even if it means upsetting her," Bambi said, pointing a Q'Bita.

"Bambi, I only got my badge back a few hours ago. Give me a chance to get out in front of this investigation before you start making a fuss."

"I haven't even begun to make a fuss, so you'd better get your tail feathers back in the game soon or I'm gonna have you plucked."

Bambi didn't even bother acknowledging Q'Bita as she stormed past.

Andy still stood in the hallway looking at her, and Q'Bita felt her cheeks warming.

"Before you start, no, I'm not proud of myself. I know that she's your past and I'm your future but she just pushes my buttons sometimes and I can't help myself."

Q'Bita could see a small smile forming on Andy's face.

"What are you smirking at?"

"Just thinking how nice it is to have two women fight over me. Feeds the old ego."

"Speaking of feeding, can we go to dinner now? I'm starving, and I have a bunch of things to tell you."

"General stuff that can be discussed over bar-b-que, or Nancy Drew stuff that's going to make me wish I had pie?"

Now it was Q'Bita's turn to smirk.

"Definitely pie."

***

Q'Bita and Andy agreed to enjoy their dinner first and talk about the case second. Technically, it was Andy's suggestion as soon as he discovered the lemon meringue pie on the dessert menu, and Q'Bita didn't have the heart to challenge him on it.

The food had been amazing, as usual, and she had just finished telling him everything she and Jamie had dug up when her phone buzzed.

"Jamie?" Andy asked.

"Actually, it's Rene. I'm guessing he got my peace offering."

"Hey, Rene."

"Don't you hey me. If you think that my forgiveness can be bought with a few paltry cookies and some flowers, then you underestimate the depth of my rage. You have wronged me, and while I have no objection to eating my feelings, you are just going to have to try harder. If I were you, I'd start by making sure that the brunch you treat me to tomorrow includes that tropical bread pudding with dark rum caramel sauce that I like. I'd insist that you have it ready for breakfast, but I'll be too busy being beside myself with grief while your intended hauls my husband off to jail. It will be at least 11 a.m. before I've recovered enough to eat. Mango Bellinis would also be a nice touch."

Q'Bita didn't get a word in before Rene hung up.

"Guess he's still mad?" Andy asked.

"Actually, he's fine. He pretended to be offended while demanding brunch. Letting me feed him is his way of accepting my apology. It's what we do."

"Good. I'd hate to have the Scooby Gang break up. I just might need your help solving this case."

Chapter 18

Early the next morning Andy and Q'Bita made their way to the kitchen to join her family for a breakfast meeting. After the meeting, Andy and Beecher would head to the station, and Beecher would be booked. Q'Bita's feet felt like they were made of heavy stone as she shuffled toward what she was sure was going to be an unpleasant scene.

She was surprised to hear laughing as they got closer to the kitchen.

"Well, it sounds like business as usual in there. Maybe this won't be so bad, after all," Andy said.

"Definitely not what I expected. I'm guessing Rene isn't here yet."

Andy held open the door and Q'Bita walked in to find her entire family, as well as Evie, Jamie, and Hadleigh, all huddled together, having coffee and muffins. The conversation ground to an uncomfortable halt as soon as they saw Q'Bita and Andy. Thankfully, her nana broke the silence quickly.

"Good morning, you two. Pull up a stool and get you some breakfast."

"Q'Bita can have breakfast. Judas Iscariot can just go back in the pantry and get himself cold cereal. These muffins are for family, not traitors."

"Rene, what have we discussed?"

Q'Bita held her breath as she watched the back-and-forth between her brother and his husband. This was the explosion she'd been expecting—she just hoped it didn't get too ugly.

"Fine. Andrew, you may partake of a muffin if you wish, but just know that because of your treachery, they were made with hands that will soon be cramped and chaffed from clutching a tear-soaked, 800-thread count Egyptian cotton handkerchief."

Andy gave Q'Bita a 'help me' look.

"Rene, it was very nice of you to make breakfast for everyone," Q'Bita said sweetly.

"I was afraid if I left it up to you, everything would be tainted with the taste of bitter betrayal."

"Rene. I thought we agreed that you were not going to overreact, and that we were going to be polite and cordial this morning," Beecher said.

"Okay, fine, we'll do it your way but I'm still angry at these two, and if this doesn't all get resolved before lunch, I cannot be responsible for my actions."

"Now, princess, don't go getting your panties all wadded up. I didn't come over there this morning just to see your puss," Evie said.

"Not to make matters worse, but I was kind of wondering why you were here myself. I thought you'd still be at the hospital with Cane," Andy said.

"Cane's doing fine, and there's something he wanted me to tell you, Andy."

The kitchen suddenly got even quieter than when Q'Bita and Andy had first walked in.

"Cane says that right before he got hit he looked up at the ridgeline to get a sense of where they were and saw Beecher about 200 yards out in front of them. He swears there's no way Beecher could have been the one to shoot that bolt."

"Oh, sweet baby Ruth, I—"

"Hush, Rene. Let the grown folk talk."

"It's okay, Liddy Lou, Rene's right; this is good news. If Cane's willing to give me a sworn statement, I can hold off on taking Beecher in for now," Andy said.

"For now? What does that mean? Are you saying that Beecher might still be arrested?" Rene asked.

"No, but there's a bunch of evidence that points to Beecher and I need to figure out why that is."

"Can't evidence be wrong?" Hadleigh asked.

"Ya, I suppose it can, but Clarity Fessler is one of the best techs I've ever worked with and it's not like her to be so far off the mark. What she came up with was pretty solid stuff."

"I thought Clarity was part of the hunt group. If she was there when this happened, can she even legally work the case?" Jamie asked.

"She ended up having to work and didn't make it to the hunt. I know she was disappointed, but it turned out to be lucky for us, because I wouldn't want anyone else collecting or handling the evidence in this case," Andy said.

Andy gave Q'Bita a kiss on top of the head and reached for a muffin.

"Probably best if I just take this to go. I'm going to grab Mikey then head over to the hospital. Tom, can you call Kent Haskell and let him know what's going on and see if he can stall Judge Tanner until I talk to Cane?"

"What about Beecher?" Rene asked.

Andy stopped part-way to the door and turned back.

"Beecher, I hate to ask, but can you stay put until I get with Judge Tanner?"

Rene reached across the table, picked up another muffin and handed it to Andy.

"Here, take two. They're small, and the more energy you have the faster this can all be resolved."

Andy winked at Q'Bita then thanked Rene.

"Don't think for one second that this means you don't have to make me brunch, Q'Bita. I realize now that Andy was just doing his job but you had no excuse. Adding copious amounts of bacon to the menu may just absolve you of your crimes against our relationship, and it had better be extra crispy but not blackened."

"What's the matter, Queenie, you go something against Cajun food?" Evie taunted.

And just like that, everything seemed to be back to normal, at least for now. Q'Bita only hoped it stayed that way for a few hours.

***

After they'd finished their breakfast and everyone had cleared out of the kitchen, Q'Bita got busy making brunch. Cooking was the one thing that had always soothed her soul. Something about the quiet solitude of an empty kitchen and the rhythmic motion of chopping and slicing just infused her with a sense of calm when everything else around her was in chaos.

She went to the pantry and grabbed dried apricots, papayas, sour cherries and a bottle of Gosling's Black Seal dark rum. Its hints of vanilla and candied fruit paired well with the tropical flavors in this recipe, and a small shot for the chef was just the little guilty pleasure she needed right now. If a little nip here and there was good enough for Julia Child, it was good enough for her.

She diced the dried fruit and gave it a soak in a few tablespoons of the Gosling's to rehydrate it then went to the walk-in to fetch her wet ingredients. On the way back she pulled the perfectly toasted challah bread out of the oven and sat it on the counter until she was ready to tear it. The key to a perfect bread pudding was in the bread itself. It needed to absorb the custard but still hold its structure, and nothing worked better than challah in Q'Bita's opinion.

She was mixing the custard when Jamie came back into the kitchen.

"Hey, Q'B-Doll, what's shaking?"

"Hey, Jamie. Did Hadleigh leave already?"

"Ya, she headed back to the office. She wouldn't admit it but this whole thing with Beecher had her all worked up. They're in the middle of negotiating a huge retail deal for the Macie Dixon Line and she's worried about what will happen if Beecher gets arrested. I guess we all are, really."

"Well, hopefully it won't come to that."

"I hope you're right, Q'Bita."

"Okay, I've known you long enough to know when you're up to something. Wanna tell me what you're up to?"

"Man, you're good. I'm glad you're not a cop."

"No worries there—I could never follow all those rules. Now, spill it."

"I know that Andy has been pretty good about looking the other way while I do a little hacking here and there, and I don't want to take advantage of that, but something's been bothering me since this all started. I kind of need to go behind his back to check into it and I was hoping you'd say it was okay."

"Jamie, I trust your gut, and as long as it helps clear Beecher, you have my blessing to do whatever you need to do. But do not get caught."

"Girl, please—"

"Yes, I know, you got skillz. It's not your skills that worry me, it's what nana will do to me if you get in trouble again."

"She'd flay us both."

"Exactly, so be careful."

Once Jamie was gone, Q'Bita finished putting together the bread pudding and got it in the oven. She carefully toasted a batch of coconut and made the dark rum caramel sauce then decided to go one step further and make some crème anglaise for added decadence.

She had just pulled the bacon off the griddle when Evie and her nana came into the kitchen.

"Hello, darling. Mind if we make a pot of tea before we head to the hospital?"

"Not at all. Why don't you two sit down, and I'll put on the water and grab some cookies?"

"Thank you, Q'Bita. I could use a little comfort cookie before I get back there and have to deal with more of Miss Crystal," Evie moaned.

"I thought Cane broke things off with her."

"Oh, he did, but now that she knows her mama ain't dying and there won't be no insurance check coming, she's been back, sniffing around Cane, trying to convince him that baby's his."

Q'Bita stopped halfway to the stove and rushed back to the table.

"Evie, did you just say something about an insurance check?"

"Lord, yes, you know how dramatic she and her mama are. Bambi was convinced she was dying of cancer last week, and Crystal had her all but dead and buried. The greedy minx even went to see Bob Franklin to find out how quick she could get her grubby hands on Bambi's insurance money. Turns out it was nothing more than a bladder infection. I curse the day my Cane ever got involved with that tramp."

"Damn. That's what I get for trusting Hilde Sanders."

"What's wrong, Q'Bita?" Liddy Lou asked.

"Hilde told me about Crystal's visit to Bob Franklin. Between that and hearing that Cane had broken things off with her, I jumped to the conclusion that maybe Crystal was somehow behind all this. It made more sense than Beecher being the shooter. I guess I'd better call Andy and let him know that he has one less suspect to present to Judge Tanner."

Andy took the news better than Q'Bita had anticipated. Cane had given him a full statement that seemed to exonerate Beecher, at least for now, but it still didn't explain the evidence or point to who the shooter was. Until they resolved that, there was still the possibility that Beecher would get the blame."

Q'Bita excused herself and went to find Jamie. She found him in the office, hunched over his laptop. He was so focused on what he was doing that he didn't even know she'd come in.

"What's so fascinating?"

Jamie jumped and gave her an annoyed look.

"Crap on a cracker, Q'Bita. You scared the hell out of me."

"I doubt that. There's probably too much hell in you to ever completely leave your body."

"Very funny. I'm working here, in case you hadn't noticed."

"That's why I'm here. Evie just blew Crystal off the suspect list. I need you to focus everything you've got on Hank Morgan. If he isn't our guy, then we need to start considering the thought that Cane wasn't the target and Put was. I pray we don't have to go down that road, because I can't imagine how long that suspect list would be, and it would put Beecher right back at the top of the list."

"As usual, I'm already a step ahead of you. I think I found something that might help with that, but your luv chicken isn't going to like it."

Jamie turned his laptop around so Q'Bita could see the screen. On it was an article about the man that Put had turned in to the EPA for taking bribes. At the top was a picture of the man and his wife and daughter walking into court for his hearing.

"I'm not sure I understand how this helps, Jamie."

"Q'Bita, look closely at the picture. Does the daughter look familiar to you at all?"

Q'Bita pinched the screen to enlarge the picture and gasped.

"Oh my God, it looks like Clarity Fessler."

"Bingo. Her real name is Clarity Conrad. Fessler is her mother's maiden name."

"Before I call Andy, are you one hundred percent sure about this, Jamie?"

"Two hundred percent sure. I felt like something was off since the beginning, when she was able to find all that evidence pointing to Beecher in less than a day. She claims to have talked to a company in Utah that gave her purchase info. It just didn't add up. Utah is three hours behind us, and she knew this by 9 a.m. our time. No way she talked to someone on the phone. That means she either hacked their records or she lied. I checked. No one hacked their records; I'd be able to tell."

Q'Bita grabbed her cell phone and called Andy. He was a little argumentative at first but came around eventually. He told her to keep a lid on this until he figured out what to do.

The next few hours were sheer torture. She hated keeping secrets from her family and almost blurted out everything during brunch but managed to somehow get through it. When Andy finally arrived back at the Red Herring, it was almost dinner time and he looked exhausted.

"I know you're chomping at the bit to know what happened but can it wait until I've had a slice of pie and a beer?"

"Wow, pie *and* beer? This must be a hell of a story."

Q'Bita had been keeping a chocolate stout ice box pie on reserve for a special occasion but this seemed like the right time to pull it out. She cut the pie in fourths and pulled two ice-cold beers from the walk-in. She stuck a fork in one of the slices and set it down in front of Andy, along with one of the beers.

He polished off the first slice and half the beer without looking up then let out a less than graceful burp.

"Man, today sucked. Y'all will be glad to know that all charges against Beecher have been dropped. Orvis and I confronted Clarity and she broke down and admitted everything. She never meant to hurt Cane; she was aiming for Put. I just can't believe this is how it all turned out. She seemed like such a smart kid, with her whole life in front of her."

Q'Bita stayed quiet and let Andy talk.

"I know that what she did was wrong, and innocent people got hurt, but I still can't help feeling sorry for her."

"Maybe it's because you see yourself in her, Andy."

"Q'Bita, don't be ridiculous. I might lose my temper once in a while but I'd never try to kill anyone."

"That's not what I'm saying. I just mean that you understand what it's like to have a parent taken from you and to want justice for what happened. That kind of hurt either breaks you or makes you stronger. The two of you took different paths down the same road."

Andy was quiet for a minute and then drained the last of his beer.

"I see what you're saying and I appreciate it. You're a smart woman, and I'm glad you and I found each other on that road."

Q'Bita reached out and squeezed Andy's hand.

"Me too."

She let Andy finish another slice of pie while she grabbed him another beer. When she got back she could hear Rene and Beecher coming across the driveway. Andy looked up at her and smiled.

"I guess we'd better tell everyone the good news… but I'm not sharing this pie."

Epilogue

Two days later everything was mostly back to normal. Rene and Evie were bickering over some soap opera while her nana ignored them both and did most of the prep work for that night's class. Q'Bita was going over the reservations for the following week with Jamie and was happy to see they had a full inn, which meant Alain would either need to find somewhere else to stay or remain in the barn until he returned to France.

Cane and Henri were both being released from hospital, and Q'Bita was thrilled that Henri and Mariah would be staying at the Red Herring Inn for another week or two until Henri was strong enough to travel. She had become so attached to them that she hated the thought of them leaving.

Andy was finally settling back in as Sheriff but was still trying to figure out how to help Clarity without upsetting everyone involved. Q'Bita loved that he cared so much about doing what was right, a quality that was sorely lacking in Alain.

Her cell phone buzzed on the desk with a text from her mother. She almost jumped out of her chair with excitement when she read, "Deal's done. Tell Andy your father was wrong. We actually got six zeros."

Once the initial excitement wore off, Q'Bita realized that life had just thrown them a curve ball that opened the door to a whole new world. She just hoped it didn't include any more drama. They'd certainly all had their fair share for a while.

Her daydreams of better things to come were cut short as Alain appeared in the office doorway.

"Q'Bita, might we have a word, please?"

"Alain, if this about the loft again, don't bother. Jamie and I were just going over the reservations and we're fully booked. If you need to stay in Castle Creek any longer you'll have to find somewhere else to stay."

Alain gave her a hurt look, which only annoyed her more.

"If I didn't know better I'd think you didn't want me here."

"You do know better, and I don't want you here. The only thing I want from you is a divorce. There's really, honestly, nothing else you have to offer me that I'd want."

Q'Bita felt her brunch churning as that look of smug confidence came over Alain's face. It was the look that he usually got just before he dropped a bomb shell on her.

"Is that so, darling? What if I told you that I just happen to have some vital information that will change everything you and your family know about what happened to your grandfather the night he died?"

There is was. The bomb shell. Alain chuckled and Q'Bita fought the urge to cry as she realized Alain wouldn't be going anywhere any time soon.

Blackberry Rosemary Simple Syrup

In the recipe section of *Sinister Cinnamon Buns* I provided a recipe for *The Simple Art of Simple Syrup* featuring rosemary. This recipe is similar, but much like Q'Bita's adventures, it's been taken to the next level with the addition of my favorite summer fruit, blackberries.

Rosemary grows like crazy in my garden so it's often my go-to choice for simple syrup, but blackberries pair well with just about any herb so feel free to substitute whatever you have on hand. Mint, basil, oregano, sage, or shiso would all be lovely and refreshing.

Q'Bita loves to add a tablespoon or two of this syrup to iced tea but it would also be fabulous over ice cream, mixed into or drizzled over cream cheese, or added to your favorite summer cocktail.

Be forewarned, this is not a recipe for which you'll want to use your cherished grandmother's wooden spoon or make it while wearing your Sunday best, as blackberries will stain anything they come in contact with.

12 oz blackberries, washed
1/2 cup white sugar
juice of 1 medium lime
1/8 teaspoon kosher salt
generous pinch of Asian five-spice powder (optional, but so worth it)
sprig of fresh rosemary, washed but left whole, and given a few bangs with the back of a chef's knife

Combine blackberries, sugar and lime juice in a medium, non-stick sauce pan. Bring to a low boil (just a smidge past a simmer) over medium heat. Stir or whisk continuously to avoid scorching the sugar. When bubbles begin to break the surface, add the salt, five-spice powder, and rosemary. Give a few quick stirs, and remove from the heat. The syrup will thicken as it cools.

Let the syrup cool to room temperature and then pour the syrup through a fine mesh strainer into a glass jar with lid or an airtight container. The blackberries are full of seeds, so you may need to press the pulp with the back of a large spoon to really get all the juice out.

Yields approximately 1 cup and can be stored in the refrigerator for two weeks.

Pepperoni Rolls

If you've ever taken a trip to West Virginia or South-Western Pennsylvania, then you've most likely encountered the *Pepperoni Roll*. They're the official state food of West Virginia, and there are as many versions of this recipe as there are Bigfoot sightings in Appalachia. I wouldn't be surprised to find out that the big furry guy is a fan of these tasty treats, too.

Pepperoni Rolls were created so coal miners could enjoy a quick, easy meal during their work day. I'm a fan of quick and easy, so I see no reason to get fancy with blue-collar food. If you have the time and the desire to make your own yeast dough recipe, then I applaud your talent and initiative, but I've gone a slightly faster route. These babies are just so good I didn't have the willpower to wait for my own dough to rise.

1 dozen frozen yeast dinner rolls (I used Rhodes brand, 36 count bag. The unused rolls keep well in the freezer)
1 6.5 oz stick of Boar's Head natural casing pepperoni (usually found in the deli section), sliced into ¼ inch rounds
½ stick melted butter
1 tablespoon Italian seasoning
flour for dusting work surface and rolling pin
small bowl or cup of water for sealing dough seams

Place the frozen dinner rolls on a sheet tray that has been sprayed with cooking spray. Cover with plastic wrap that has also been sprayed with cooking spray. Let dough thaw, approximately 1 hour or until pliable and ready to be rolled out.

Preheat over to 350 degrees Fahrenheit.

Lightly flour your work surface, hands, and rolling pin. You don't want to overdo it with the flour or you'll end up with tough dough. Pull dough into a rectangle approximately 3 inches by 4 inches and then place on floured work surface and roll to ¼ inch thickness.

Place 3-4 slices of pepperoni down the center of your rectangle, overlapping slices slightly. Don't skimp on the pepperoni, but also keep in mind that you will need to leave about a ¼ inch lip on all sides so you can close your roll. If you're going to add cheese (see note), now would be the time to do so.

Dip your index finger in the water and rub a tiny bit around the edges of the dough, then carefully bring the long sides of the dough together and pinch to seal the seam. Tuck in the open ends and pinch to seal those as well.

Place sealed roll on a baking pan that has been sprayed with cooking spray. Place the rolls approximately 2-3 inches apart as they'll expand as they bake.

When you've finished all 12 rolls, spray a piece of plastic wrap with cooking spray and cover the rolls. Set the rolls aside and let them rest/rise for approximately 30 minutes.

While the rolls are rising, melt butter in a small sauce pan then remove from heat and stir in the Italian seasoning.

When the rolls are finished rising, brush tops and sides with a small amount of the seasoned butter then bake for 15-20 minutes, until cooked through and golden-brown on top.

Note: Some purists insist that a Pepperoni Roll is just dough and meat, but there are other camps who add cheese, and even others who add peppers and sauce. When I tested this recipe, I added a bit of shredded mozzarella on top of my pepperoni slice, but I have to be honest, it was a pain to roll with little shreds of cheese going everywhere. If you want to add cheese, I would suggest using sliced mozzarella or provolone.

Condolence Casserole

Condolence Casserole is a term I made up for this book but it seems to fit nicely with the idea of southern hospitality and funeral etiquette I imagine my characters would possess. If you've ever lost a loved one, you know how comforting it can be to see a smiling face on your doorstep, bearing a covered dish.

These are dishes made with love and sympathy and are meant to comfort a wounded soul. They don't need to be fussy or complicated. In fact, the more simple and familiar, the better. Think warm, gooey dishes that can easily go from fridge or freezer, to the oven, and then to the table with as little effort and clean-up as possible.

The recipe that follows is one that I think truly embraces the concept of the perfect Condolence Casserole. It pairs well with ham and works equally well as a dessert.

3-4 cups of egg bread (challah or brioche work well for this recipe), cut into one-inch cubes
1 ½ cups of white sugar
3 large eggs, beaten
1 cup of heavy cream or half-and-half (for something different consider using canned coconut milk)
½ cup of melted butter, divided
1 20 oz can of crushed pineapple with juice
1 teaspoon of vanilla
½ teaspoon of cinnamon (can also use Asian five-spice powder or speculaas)

Preheat oven to 350 degrees.
Set aside 2 tablespoons of the melted butter then combine all ingredients except bread in a large mixing bowl. Mix well to combine all ingredients. Add bread to bowl in batches and mix gently until all the bread has been

thoroughly incorporated into the wet ingredients. Be careful not to break the bread up too much while mixing.

Pour mixture into a 13x9-inch baking dish that has been greased or sprayed with cooking spray. Drizzle remaining melted butter over the top of the casserole and bake 30-45 minutes until well-set and golden-brown on top.

About J Lee Mitchell

J Lee Mitchell is the author of The Red Herring Inn Mystery series and the soon to be released Critic in the City Mystery series. She does her writing, cooking, and gardening in the heart of South Central Pennsylvania's Amish Country.

When she's not doing these things, she writes horror, zombie fiction, and dreams of training ninjas.

She enjoys traveling, quilting, hoarding cookbooks, and spending time with the World's most patient and loving significant other.

Visit J Lee Mitchell at jleemitchell.com, sign up to her newsletter, and connect with her via Facebook:
https://www.facebook.com/RedHerringInn/

Also By J Lee Mitchell

Red Herring Inn Mysteries

Sinister Cinnamon Buns

Moonshine and Malice

Acknowledgements

This book would not have been possible without the guidance, encouragement, and talent of some very wonderful people. I am forever grateful and in debt to you all.

Thank you to my family. Your love and crazy antics have given me more inspiration than a dozen writers could use in a lifetime.

Thank you, RE Vance, for being the best coach and mentor any writer could hope to have.

Thank you, Micki K Jordan, for always listening, caring, and pushing me to work harder.

Thank you, Ella Medler, for your excellent feedback and editing.

Thank you, Mariah Sinclair, for designing fabulous covers.

Thank you, Katie Sue Chaffin for being my official West Virginia consultant and favorite Luv Chicken.

Thank you, all of my SPS FoF peeps. You guys are the best motivation an author can have.

Last, but never least, thank you, Bob. Everything I do is only possible because of all the love and support you give me each and every day. You're the best friend and partner a girl could ever have.

CPSIA information can be obtained
at www.ICGtesting.com
Printed in the USA
LVHW112132271022
731790LV00019B/240